P9-DMA-044

"You do realize you're challenging me," Troy said

"Mmm-hmm." Miranda stepped toward him, closing the mere inches between them. His bold wife knew just what he wanted then. He recognized the flare of desire in her eyes, sensed in that moment he'd accomplished his goal by distracting her big-time.

There was nothing between them except a growing erotic challenge. She wanted him to beg. He wanted her to beg. It was a potent combination. And with the variety of sex toys around them, he thought they both stood a good chance of getting what they wanted.

Miranda slipped out of his arms in a playful move he hadn't been prepared for, leaving him feeling the sudden distance between them, but he didn't complain.

Not when she slipped her curly mane over her shoulder and reached for her zipper...then Troy braced himself for the show that was about to begin.

Blaze™

Dear Reader,

The FALLING INN BED... miniseries has been all about exploring how falling in bed leads to falling in love. So far we've savored the sweetness of *finally* giving in to long-term lust. We've grown breathless with sparks-at-first-sight. Now let me introduce my already-in-progress couple (a phrase borrowed from talented Harlequin Temptation author Tanya Michaels—thanks, Tanya!).

Miranda and Troy have known what they wanted from each other from the moment they met—to be together in and out of bed. But saying "I do!" isn't always enough to ensure a happily ever after. Luckily for these two, love forms a solid foundation for marriage and lust proves an effective tool for tackling even daunting obstacles.

I hope *Pillow Chase* brings you to happily ever after. Let me know. Drop me a line in care of Harlequin Books, 225 Duncan Mill Road, Don Mills, Ontario Canada M3B 3K9, or visit my Web site at www.jeanielondon.com.

Very truly yours,

Jeanie London

Books by Jeanie London

HARLEQUIN BLAZE

*Falling Inn Bed...

PILLOW CHASE

Jeanie London

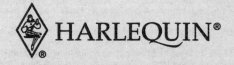

TORONTO • NEW YORK • LONDON
AMSTERDAM • PARÍS • SYDNEY • HAMBURG
STOCKHOLM • ATHENS • TOKYO • MILAN • MADRID
PRAGUE • WARSAW • BUDAPEST • AUCKLAND

If you purchased this book without a cover you should be aware
that this book is stolen property. It was reported as "unsold and
destroyed" to the publisher, and neither the author nor the
publisher has received any payment for this "stripped book."

To Quinta and Edward Flood, a very special couple who
are living proof that love can conquer anything. You've
shared your lives for more than sixty years, and I thank you
for sharing the past twenty-two with me. Love you both!

ISBN 0-373-79165-8

PILLOW CHASE

Copyright © 2004 by Jeanie LeGendre.

All rights reserved. Except for use in any review, the reproduction or
utilization of this work in whole or in part in any form by any electronic,
mechanical or other means, now known or hereafter invented, including
xerography, photocopying and recording, or in any information storage
or retrieval system, is forbidden without the written permission of the
publisher, Harlequin Enterprises Limited, 225 Duncan Mill Road,
Don Mills, Ontario, Canada M3B 3K9.

All characters in this book have no existence outside the imagination of
the author and have no relation whatsoever to anyone bearing the same
name or names. They are not even distantly inspired by any individual
known or unknown to the author, and all incidents are pure invention.

This edition published by arrangement with Harlequin Books S.A.

® and TM are trademarks of the publisher. Trademarks indicated with
® are registered in the United States Patent and Trademark Office, the
Canadian Trade Marks Office and in other countries.

www.eHarlequin.com

Printed in U.S.A.

Prologue

IF EVER A WOMAN had been born to make a man think of sex, that woman was his wife, Miranda. And if ever a hotel had been designed to make Lieutenant Commander Troy Knight imagine the variety of ways to make love to his bride of barely two years, it was Falling Inn Bed, and Breakfast.

This hotel had won the Most Romantic Getaway Award with good reason. Ever since they'd visited during the planning stages of their wedding, Troy had been impressed by how this hotel's amenities focused on couples. Shops offered everything from sex toys to lingerie, and the brand-new Wedding Wing kicked off its grand opening with a large-scale promotional campaign called the Naughty Nuptials.

And then there were all these romance-themed suites.

The one spreading out before him now was an aphrodisiac of sight and sound, so exotic that Troy could only stand beside Miranda in the doorway and take it all in.

Purple silk veils draped gold furnishings. Statues of couples in erotic poses doubled as columns to separate the living and dining areas. Vases and screens made of colored stones. Sultry flute and cymbal music. Swaying rattan fans.

The Egyptian Pleasure Pyramid.

Whoever named this suite hadn't been kidding.

A domed wall and ceiling of glass made up the far end of the room. Beyond lay a courtyard of foliage and flowers and bright summer sky. A garden oasis in the middle of gilded opulence. And this would be their home for the next three weeks.

Troy couldn't stop smiling and didn't bother to try. He pushed the door wide and motioned Miranda inside, appreciating the sight of her from this vantage. Slim and feminine, she moved with a sensual grace that always caught him hard. Even the black curls tumbling down her back made him think about how all that silky hair felt on his skin.

When he'd married her in an elaborate ceremony in this very hotel nearly two years ago, Troy hadn't realized that his desire for her could grow any stronger. He'd guessed marriage would satisfy his hunger and make them more comfortable together.

In some ways it had, but marriage hadn't dulled the ache inside that pushed him to shut this door and keep her all to himself until they had to return to the real world.

That ache still took him by surprise. The feeling was potent, *urgent,* as if he couldn't get enough time with his wife and wanted to make the most of every second together.

Troy knew this feeling intimately. As a career naval officer, he'd experienced his share of situations where urgency kept him alive. To return to Miranda.

"So what do you think of our suite, Mrs. Knight?" He closed the door and shut out the world.

"I'm not sure what to think."

Her silky voice started his pulse humming, and he covered the distance to where she stood inspecting their surroundings, eyes wide and kissable lips parted. Plucking the purse from her hand, Troy hung it on the back of a chair. "This suite looks like the Web site."

"Only in real-time."

Her voice gave no clue whether she thought real-time was a good thing, so he lifted her stylish hat away to free up his view. Just a glimpse, and Troy recognized the distance in her expression, the shadows in her gaze.

Real-time should have been a *great* thing. Three weeks together in a romance resort after months spent apart during his latest deployment should have been better than great.

But Miranda's closed expression suggested otherwise. He recognized the look—one she wore in public—a beautiful, perfect mask that showed no hint what she felt inside.

Miranda excelled at dealing socially with his commanding officers. She was the envy of his peers, and Troy enjoyed having her on his arm during the many functions that were as much a part of his career as his special operations missions. He'd been reared military and understood the game. To others, his wife was an extension of him, half of the whole. He was very proud of her.

But Troy loved Miranda best when she let her hair down and looked eager. She didn't look eager now. She looked…unreadable. Her public persona was firmly in place, her expression so remote he'd have needed a nuclear sub to maneuver the distance to his wife. The wife he knew was in there. *Somewhere.*

He had three weeks to find her.

"Who knew they could come up with a suite wilder than the Roman Bagnio?" he said, a reminder of the romance-themed suite they'd enjoyed on their wedding night not so long ago.

"Those baths were definitely wild."

Folding her in his arms, he drank in the feel of her smooth curves, warm and familiar and inviting. "Definitely wild. This time we'll be around here long enough to put these facilities to good use."

"Our wedding night wasn't enough for you last time, Lieutenant Commander?"

"Not even close."

They'd been the last couple to be married at Falling Inn Bed before construction had started on the new Wedding Wing. Now that the addition to the historic hotel was finally complete, they'd been invited back to participate in the inaugural events as the featured honeymoon couple.

Troy had been all for this vacation. The ongoing war against terrorism had been demanding his attention through most of their marriage. While separation was a normal part of their life together—he'd been stationed in Norfolk pre-9/11 when they'd met—regular deployment into the action had been keeping him away more than usual.

A lot more than was healthy for any relationship.

Troy couldn't say if the separation was a problem. He and Miranda didn't argue. They weren't angry with each other or disappointed with anything but the length of time they spent apart. Yet lately whenever he returned from a mission, it took longer and longer to find her behind that perfect wife persona she wore in public.

He thought she might be dealing with some wartime anxiety issues, but she'd assured him that his e-mail posts and phone calls kept her stress manageable. As far as she was concerned, they'd always dealt with separation. She pointed out how his mother had a husband and two children serving various functions in the armed forces right now. If he wasn't worried about how his mother coped, he shouldn't be worried about her.

Troy could only take her at her word. No stranger to a demanding lifestyle, Miranda was part of a politically active family, which came with a set of demands as unique as his own. She could maneuver the territory.

Yet he couldn't shake the feeling that this woman who meant everything to him was quietly retreating behind an invisible wall. Or that the intimacy, which had always been such an amazing part of their relationship, was slipping away. Troy might not be sure what the problem was, but there was a problem. He felt it down deep.

He had three weeks to get Miranda to share whatever was bothering her.

And Falling Inn Bed, and Breakfast happened to be the perfect place to carry out that mission objective. This hotel specialized in couples, and when they were together, the rest of the world ceased to exist, which was exactly what needed to happen so they could focus on what was really important.

Each other.

1

WHO KNEW A BLINDFOLD would make such a difference?

Miranda Knight hadn't, but with one silk scarf throwing the world into shadow, her remaining senses were heightened, lending the oncoming sexual encounter an unfamiliar thrill.

Since arriving for their stint as the Hottest Honeymoon Couple at the Wedding Wing's grand opening, she'd made lots of discoveries, both in her sexual fantasies and otherwise. With Troy, the fantasies were always well worth the effort.

Regrettably the *otherwise* hadn't been so accommodating.

But right now Miranda wasn't going to think about anything but her fantasies. The *otherwise* had no place intruding in her thoughts when she sat on a chaise in the Egyptian Pleasure Pyramid oasis, blindfolded, with a whole morning ahead to enjoy her husband.

Troy was an early bird who opened his eyes fully awake. She had to work harder to face the day, always worth facing whenever Troy twined his arms around hers and kissed her until pleasure made her gladly swap dreams for reality.

Lovemaking in the afternoon could be equally gratifying. Sometimes they wore themselves out and wound up napping in each other's arms. Other times they worked up such an appetite that dinner became a meal best served in bed, where they didn't have to dress or make polite conversation with Troy's commanding officers or the other men on his team.

She liked making love with him late at night, too. When the lights went out, she used her hands to see, to take control and drive Troy wild. His throaty growls would echo in the darkness, and that was her favorite way to fall asleep, feeling adored and satisfied and so very pleased with herself.

When Miranda really got down to it, she liked making love with her handsome husband anytime, anywhere.

Good thing, too, because right now she needed a good diversion. The *otherwise* had been stressful in ways she hadn't expected. She'd meant for this vacation to be a break from reality, a chance to reacquaint themselves after so many months apart. Coming back to Falling Inn Bed was supposed to help her focus on them as a couple and forget all about the stresses of their everyday lives.

Not to mention that Niagara Falls was home, and Miranda had been counting on feeling better once back on familiar turf.

Unfortunately geography didn't seem to be making the difference. They were two weeks into their trip—the grand opening's official Hottest Honeymoon week would begin tomorrow—and she was sitting here half-naked, blindfolded and *thinking*.

Thankfully the beep of the microwave distracted her, and Miranda frowned into her dark world, wondering what Troy was up to. He'd seemed interested in a lot more than food this morning. She hadn't heard him sneak up behind her while she'd been dressing. He'd scooped her into his arms and brought her out to this oasis then left her sitting here, waiting.

Stretching back on the chaise, Miranda let her hair spread around her in a pose she hoped would entice the man from his meal. She wasn't going to think about food while basking in this unfamiliar awareness of her senses.

In her mind's eye she could see the oasis, alive with blossoms and lush foliage, smells that grew thick in the warmth of the morning sun. Gardenia, jasmine, rose, lily and, beneath others she couldn't name, the rich scent of earth.

The garden fanned out around a small tiled piazza. A fountain with whimsical sculptures of a naked couple filled this oasis with the steady bubbling of water. Hidden audio speakers piped music through the suite, the soft strains of a tambourine, cymbals and flute weaving an exotic tune that lent to the fantasy of the place.

Rattan fans circulated air over her bare skin and, combined with the blindfold, she felt aroused in a way she'd never felt before, vulnerable almost to the point of breathlessness. And curious, too, especially when the refrigerator door opened.

What was Troy doing? Her husband was an adventurer in bed on a normal day, always cherishing and challenging her, but with him so caught up in the spirit of the Naughty Nuptials and all the erotic events…

Miranda heard the scuff of movement across the thick oriental rugs in the living room, and suddenly her whole body felt attuned to the sounds, to the soft stir of branches as he passed into the courtyard, to the careful clatter of something—a tray perhaps—on the tiled tabletop. And then the quiet hush of his breaths when he came to stand beside her.

She could sense his presence. Chemistry connected them, an awareness on some elemental level that not even this blindfold diminished. Miranda could *feel* him, could feel his gaze sweep over her. She knew he stood beside her, most likely smiling at the sight she made spreading out on the chaise.

Marriage had only deepened their connection. She'd learned to sense Troy's moods, to guess at his thoughts behind those striking green eyes. And the phenomenon worked both ways. They didn't always need words and could often communicate with a glance or a touch. She liked that about their relationship.

Well, she usually liked it… She suspected Troy could sense something was off with her now, despite her best efforts to leave her worries back in San Diego. She wouldn't let *anything* spoil their time together, not when they had a fantasy vacation to enjoy and he'd been gone for so long.

Stretching out, she hoped to entice him, to prove how determined she was to have fun. He claimed they were soul mates, and while she honestly hadn't given much thought to her stance on traveling through lifetimes to find each other, Miranda knew only Troy had ever made her feel so aroused by simply knowing he wanted her.

And she knew he did. Even with the blindfold.

She *felt* him taking his time to peruse her, drawing

out the silence, comfortable with it. Her insides grew fluttery, her breath poised in her throat as she awaited his next move.

"I like watching your body respond to me." His voice was hard-edged and strong with no hint of an accent. "I don't even have to touch you."

Troy had been reared all over the world, a typical military brat, and the only sound that came through in his voice right now was the sound of stimulated male.

Who needed to *see* when she could *hear* how much he wanted her?

"I try to be an accommodating wife."

"You are that, Mrs. Knight. No question." Slipping his hand under her ankles, he maneuvered himself beneath her and placed her feet in his lap. "You don't know how many times I've been in my barracks falling asleep, trying to figure out what I've done to deserve you. Why are you willing to wait for me to come home when you could have a husband who's always with you?"

Troy wasn't shy about sharing how he felt, and she'd always appreciated his honesty, relied on his ability to steer them through emotional waters because she didn't find it so easy.

"You love me," she said simply.

"I do."

And he seemed committed to proving how much he loved every little part of her when he massaged her feet. Miranda inhaled deeply, a sound of pure contentment as his touch melted her muscles, and she reveled in the simple joy of togetherness. For some couples time together was a given, for them it was a gift.

Easing her foot in a circle, Troy worked the muscles

along her calves then began the process over again with the other. His fingers glided along her hose, his strong hands touching her in all the right places.

"So what have I done to deserve this special treatment?" Miranda asked.

"You love me." He dragged his mouth along her instep and warmed the silk with a kiss.

She trembled as he nibbled his way along her anklebone, an area of her body she'd never realized was so sensitive. And this wasn't the only erotic discovery she'd made since becoming involved with her husband.

Troy's sense of adventure was one of the things that had attracted her to then-Lieutenant Knight. He'd seemed larger than life, more exciting than any man she'd ever known, and it was much more than his career and his uniform. Much more than his piercing green eyes and striking blond looks. Much more than his aura of powerful male.

It was simply *him*, and his wonderful zest for living.

He made her reach beyond herself and the world she knew. He didn't have any trouble handling the visibility that came along with her family, with having a father and grandfather who were both politicians. Troy performed beautifully in public but managed to live life as if no one was watching.

It was a skill she hoped to learn.

As far as Miranda was concerned, Troy was a good influence. He'd even turned their wedding into a celebration. Scoffing at the traditional, he'd talked her into a fantasy wedding at this romance resort. Then he'd whisked her away from Niagara Falls for a life filled with travel and excitement and challenges she'd never dreamed of.

Challenges she'd never dreamed she couldn't live up to.

Squelching the thought brutally, Miranda slid her fingers through his hair. The familiar feel of the brushed short strands helped chase away her thoughts with a burst of tenderness for how much she loved this man. And how much she would do to be with him.

Like stop thinking. She wasn't supposed to be thinking.

Tracing the curl of his ear, Miranda trailed her fingers along his hairline, along the curve of his jaw beneath smoothly sculpted cheeks. She searched for the pulse beating there.

And she found it, strong and steady. Like Troy himself.

Pressing her fingers into his throat, she counted the beats, her own heart speeding its pace when he ran his tongue through that responsive hollow between anklebone and heel. He swirled his tongue over her foot, a lush stroke, before gusting a warm breath between her toes.

He made the simplest touch erotic, made her respond to him as easily. It was his gift, one that bore out his belief about soul mates.

And made her so very glad they'd found each other.

When she heard a thunk against the tabletop, she tried to distinguish the sound, but couldn't. Letting her fingers drift away from his skin, she waited.

An unexpected warmth touched the bottom of her foot, and she started, earning a throaty chuckle from Troy as he pressed the solid heat to her skin, that solid *cylindrical* heat…and she realized what he'd been nuking in the microwave.

"And I thought you were making breakfast."

He rolled the warm sex toy over the ball of her foot, over muscles he'd massaged into supple compliance. "I'm making a meal out of you. Hungry?"

"Only for you."

"Good."

"So what is this, Lieutenant Commander? The glass dildo or the see-through vibrator?" He'd obviously helped himself to some goodies from one of the more unique features of this suite.

The sexy sheet sets.

Each day housekeeping outfitted the gold-framed bed in specialty sheets with names like the Kama Sutra Sports Set and the Incredible Edible. Each set came equipped with a surplus of sexy toys for couples to play with.

"You tell me, Mrs. Knight."

"Oh, so you want to play games?"

He didn't reply, just eased the device up her calf, a two-handed move that made her sigh. But content didn't seem to be the reaction he wanted because he grazed the device lightly behind her knee.

"That tickles." She scrambled away, but didn't get far. With this blindfold, she wasn't sure where the chaise ended and didn't want to overbalance and land on the floor.

Not that Troy wouldn't save her. He'd catch her before she could go over the side, but she much preferred to look enticing in her blindfold rather than clumsy.

But her vanity came with a price, and choosing the path of least risk meant exposing the insides of her thighs. Troy zeroed in on the target, skimming that warmth along her skin, tickling her until her muscles quivered with her efforts to resist.

But he wasn't having any part of resistance.

"Spread your legs." Arousal made his voice a sexy command, and shifting around, he wedged his hips between her knees to force her to comply.

Miranda didn't need her eyesight to know hunger had sharpened the lines of his face, made him look focused, *predatory*. She'd burned that expression into her memory to carry her through the times when they were apart.

But they were together now, and using his ruthlessly toned body to best effect, Troy crowded her against the sloping back of the chaise, filled her senses with the feel of him, the familiar male scent of his freshly scrubbed skin.

He never slowed those achingly teasing touches, but worked his way toward the juncture between her thighs until his sexy device warmed the panty hose against her aroused sex.

Sliding her hands along his chest, she used touch to anchor herself as that invading heat melted her insides. She traced the broad hollows of his smooth skin, but before she could slip her arms around him, that heat between her legs burst into motion, an electronic vibration that pulsated against her most private places and made her gasp in surprise.

"Does that answer your question, Mrs. Knight?"

He pressed his mouth against her ear, breathed a sultry breath, another sensual assault that sent that surge of moist fire straight to her core.

The sensation was too unexpected, too direct, too potent, and she writhed against it, found her attempts to escape only heightened the intensity. Her stomach gathered against the pleasure. Her breasts grew heavy and tight.

"The see-through vibrator." She exhaled the words on a breath.

His low chuckle radiated against her ear, another reverberation that throbbed low in her belly. "Surprise. It's more than just a see-through vibrator."

"What is it?"

He upped the speed a notch and the humming grew louder.

"Oh, Troy." She didn't give him a chance to answer when that pulsation caught the bundle of nerve endings hidden in the folds of her sex. A shock wave ran through her.

"I'm keeping that part a surprise so you'll have something to look forward to."

"More games." The protest was pure bravado because Miranda wasn't sure she wanted another surprise, not when she couldn't decide whether to ride the palpating sensation or attempt an escape.

Troy loved doing this to her, too. He loved seeing how far he could push until she dissolved into an incoherent puddle of impulses that would do anything for satisfaction.

He also knew about paybacks. In fact, she thought he looked forward to them... But right now he was at his highly trained finest, trailing wet kisses down her jaw and neck, sucking gently at the pulse in the base of her throat, making her whole body tingle under such a sexy assault.

Her breasts had grown heavy with desire. Pulling him closer, she rasped her nipples against his chest for some relief. But her bra interfered with the friction of skin against skin, and he wouldn't shift forward enough to make a difference.

Then again, why should he move? His growing erection had inched against her thigh, and all he had to do was arch his hips to ease his own ache.

No, Troy was having a good time exactly where he was, teasing her with openmouthed kisses along her shoulder. He used the vibrator to awaken every nerve ending between her head and toes and her panty hose eased his journey between her thighs. Slipping the tip slightly inside, he explored her most intimate places, and the feel of silk-covered tip gently probing aroused her until she could only surrender to the sensation, feeling the promise of a climax lingering in the distance. Swelling, waning and *there,* just out of reach.

She wasn't the only one feeling the effects of his sexy game, either. Troy's kisses grew demanding. He trailed his mouth down her chest, toward her breasts, and for a breathless moment she thought he might grant her wish and remove her bra, but he only speared his tongue beneath the lace, barely reaching her nipple with a teasing wet stroke.

She would have removed the thing herself, but their position hindered her mobility. He kneeled over her, all warm, hard muscle and bare skin, and she could only trace the strong hollows of his chest, reveling in the tightness that was a result of his rigorous training.

Miranda could ride his erection, though. Every arch of her hips dragged her silk-clad thigh against him. She wanted him to share this urgency she felt, but Troy obviously recognized her game because the vibrator suddenly stopped.

Sucking in a deep breath, she protested with a gasp as the intense arousal ebbed its frenzied pace.

"Don't go anywhere." Propping himself up, he maneuvered out of the tangle of arms and legs they'd become. "I'm coming right back."

The gravelly rough sound of his voice made her smile. "I'm a captive audience, Lieutenant Commander. Even if you weren't sitting on my legs, I can't see to get up and leave."

He chuckled and eased off her, and Miranda blindly loosened her hair from where it had caught in her bra strap, wondering what her handsome husband had in store for her next.

She didn't wonder long. A dragging sound suddenly drowned out the throb of her heartbeat.

"What are you doing?" she asked. "Rearranging the furniture?"

"Just a chair so I can reach the next part of my surprise."

"More surprises." He hadn't finished the job from his first surprise. Her heartbeat hadn't slowed to a normal pace yet, and her bottom ached with pulsing little bursts. "Can I handle it?"

The question slipped out, proving her thoughts were still lingering too close to the surface. But Troy didn't seem to notice. He placed his hands on her waist, his *cold* hands.

With a yelp, she tried to scramble out of his reach only to find herself cornered by the back of the chaise. "Troy, I don't want a surprise that involves ice."

Laughing, he snagged the waistband of her panty hose and worked the jumble over her hips and down her legs, warming his fingers on her skin along the way. Then he disappeared again.

The blindfold that had started out adding a thrill had

become problematic. She was half tempted to remove it to prepare herself for his icy surprise, but the scent of male suddenly filled her senses. The velvet soft head of a very impressive erection brushed her cheek as Troy leaned over her.

Miranda found herself face-to-face with a perfect chance to turn the tables. Since chances this opportune didn't come along often, she struck out with her tongue and dragged a wet stroke along his hot length.

Troy exhaled hard, and that steely erection bobbed against her mouth. With a laugh, and exceptional aim for a blindfolded woman, she drew him inside in a hard pull.

His body jolted in surprise, and he slid his hand into her hair, suddenly needing to hang on.

"Miranda." A warning that she tested his restraint.

Exactly what she wanted. To test him. To tempt him. To take the upper hand. With an inspired move, she drew back and glided down his erection again.

And again.

She didn't care how hard his legs shook. He shouldn't have stuck this greedy thing anywhere near her mouth if he didn't want to deal with the consequences. Remaining on his feet was his concern, not hers, so Miranda threaded her arms around him, sank her fingers into his butt and urged him forward for a deeper stroke.

That one almost choked her, but she managed to dodge her gag reflex just in time to hear him groan. *Loud.*

He seemed undecided whether to let her take control or make a break for it, but as long as his hand was on her head *she* couldn't go anywhere. So with her mouth against his crotch, Miranda took him for a ride with long deep pulls and some lingering wet swirls of her tongue for good measure.

He lasted longer than she'd expected. Then again, Troy had been making up for lost time ever since their arrival at this hotel. His control should be well in place after that much sex, but she couldn't help laughing when he broke away, a desperate move that proved she'd almost had him.

"I'm not ready to be over," he said.

"Are you sure? I was having a good time."

"I noticed." Urging her forward, he slid onto the chaise behind her, cradling her between his spread thighs.

He was all hard muscle and warm skin as he nestled her in the curve of his body. She felt surrounded by him, that hot erection pressing against her lower back, and she savored the feel of skin against skin, appreciated being together.

Miranda missed Troy when he was away, but somehow never so much as when he came home again. Only then could she allow herself the luxury of remembering how his strong arms felt around her, how his body sheltered her in its heat, how she felt loved and cherished and so glad they were together again.

She gave a sigh, and the sound turned into a purr as he slid a hand between her legs to coax the sensitive bundle of nerve endings from its hiding place. With her panty hose gone, Miranda enjoyed the full potency of his touch as Troy idly fondled her, coiling the tension inside until she parted her thighs to increase that drive-me-wild friction that was swiftly driving her wild.

He'd always had this sort of power over her, the ability to shoot her from zero to sixty with the perfect combination of intimacy and exploration. He knew what aroused her because he'd taken the time to learn, continued to learn, continued to share his likes and explore new pleasures with her.

Each time he returned from a mission, the process began over again. They reveled in being together. They appreciated the contrast of newness and familiarity. They pleased each other in ways only they could. And right now, with this blindfold, Miranda became more aware of his touches than ever before.

That tension wound tighter as he dragged his fingers through her damp heat, and she nestled back against him, feeling the solid warmth of him surround her. She was content in the knowledge that they still had another week to play out this fantasy together. Another week to enjoy the pleasures of being together again.

"Trust me?" he whispered close to her ear as he rested his chin on her shoulder, pressed a kiss into her hair.

"With all my heart."

She'd been so preoccupied with her arousal that she hadn't felt him move, so when the first icy droplet trickled between her legs, she gasped and tried to pull away.

"Surprise." He nudged the tip against her aroused skin, a quick touch to test her response. "The see-through vibrator turned out to be a lot more."

"What—" she sucked in another hard breath, eyelids blinking against the blindfold in a rebellious attempt to see "—*is* this? A water torture device?"

"A *dual temperature* vibrator." Another quick nudge that made her sex contract wildly as the cold blasted her skin. "The extreme sensations are supposed to push you over the edge."

"I'll be over the edge of this chaise if you touch me with that thing again."

"Sure you don't want to give it a shot? You're so hot that cooling down might feel good." He used his *cool* fingers to up her temperature a few more degrees.

She might be hot, but when another droplet dripped onto her stomach and into her navel, Miranda jumped.

"How about this to help you decide?" Troy finally went for her bra, lifting the garment under her arms so her breasts tumbled free. He knew exactly how to arouse her, how to make her dissolve in his arms so she'd agree to anything.

And that was exactly what Miranda needed right now. She needed to abandon herself to arousal, wanted to drown out her thoughts with pleasure, so she couldn't think of anything but the way he rolled her nipples into a frenzy of sensation. The way he swirled the vibrator around a tip. The way the condensation chilled her, shocking in intensity.

"How's that?" he asked.

She took a few deep breaths, willed herself to relax enough to describe the feeling. As that ache speared through her, she realized that *torture* wasn't an adequate description. "It's...*different*."

"Too much?"

She shook her head. "Just intense."

Touching the tip to her other nipple, he shot the cold through her again, making her arch her back to press into his hands, to feed this icy ache.

With skilled fingers, Troy obliged. He warmed her

skin with knowing touches, and hot pleasure radiated through her, a striking contrast to the cold, an intensity that made her realize exactly what she wanted.

Curling her fingers over his hand, Miranda guided his newest toy between her thighs. "Let's try this."

She started tentatively, testing the feel of that iciness, pausing to prepare herself for each touch.

"Still intense?" He glided the vibrator lightly along her in a channel of chilly condensation and warm skin.

"Mmm-hmm, but nice. In small doses."

With the flick of a switch, he made the vibrator hum to life, the pulsation against her oh-so sensitive sex causing her to moan out loud. He rolled it against that bundle of nerves, a glancing caress that made her shiver.

"I like this." He dragged his mouth over her throat in an openmouthed kiss and pressed the length of the vibrator between her thighs, catching her everywhere with that pulsating cold.

Miranda didn't reply. She was too busy riding the sensation, and she wasn't the only one. Troy ground his erection against her back, a demand that conveyed his need louder than words. Her pleasure brought him pleasure. What could be better?

Miranda could think of only one thing.

Scooting up on his lap, she arched her bottom until his erection rode forward. She didn't have to say a word. He knew what she wanted. Slipping a hand between them, he maneuvered that hardness against her chilled skin, a hot length that sank inside with an unfamiliar force that stole her breath.

She was so tight and wet that he growled, a throaty rumble against her ear as he grasped his arms around her, gave a few driving thrusts that made her gasp. And that sexy device…he held it poised where she could feel it most, and condensation mingled chilly water with their body's heat to create a powerful sensation that had her rocking back to meet his thrusts.

Only Troy could take her apart this way, could overwhelm her with his body, with his hunger, with his love. He indulged her, took his own enjoyment in her responses, and the simple honesty of his emotions, the *overwhelming* honesty urged her to reply in kind, to coax him into the same frenzy.

And Miranda could always satisfy her husband in bed. She was an accommodating wife, the perfect match to her equally accommodating husband.

So why had life become such a struggle?

The question sideswiped her, a rational thought that cut through her haze of pleasure, *real.* And the special connection they shared betrayed her. Troy must have sensed her hesitation, guessed she'd become distracted, because he suddenly slowed his pace to press hungry kisses along her neck.

She didn't want anything to intrude on their time together, especially not thoughts that had no place in their bed. So arching her head back, she leaned into his touch, reassured by the feel of his mouth on her skin, the way he could turn unwanted doubts into breathless gasps.

His every stroke combined with the vibrator, so direct, so intense, so overwhelming, and she forced her focus onto the way her sex clenched in greedy reply, so close to the edge.

Holding her breath expectantly, she tried to knead her climax into breaking, wanting to lose herself in the ecstasy she knew in Troy's arms, needing oblivion to drown out the thoughts racing inside her head.

But the sensation remained just beyond reach. Even though her body burned. Even though she wanted release so much that she clung to her husband and rode him with hard strokes. Even though she tried to crowd out the intruding thoughts by the strength of her will and the blinding force of their lovemaking.

Despite the effort, her oncoming orgasm evaporated like a mist beneath the sun. Within the space of a heartbeat, all her pleasure slipped away, leaving behind only a lingering warmth to mock her.

It was gone, and wouldn't come back. No matter how hard Miranda willed herself to relax. No matter how far she'd already traveled toward fulfillment. No matter how she yearned to feel her husband's hands on her. The moment was over no matter what Troy might do to arouse her again.

For one blind moment she thought about admitting her climax had gotten away. It happened. All couples faced an ebb and flow of arousal when they'd been together a while. This shouldn't be a big deal, wouldn't have been…

Except this wasn't the first time.

2

TROY HAD MIRANDA on the verge of coming apart in his arms and then in an instant, he'd lost her. Bonelessness had yielded to stillness. Frenzied reactions had become deliberate.

He'd been making love to his wife for a long time and knew neither of them could always be on. Miranda knew that, too. But instead of giving him a chance to find other ways to arouse her or at least being honest about losing the mood, she'd distracted him. She'd kickstarted a rhythm he hadn't been able to resist.

She'd pretended everything was all right.

It wasn't. They had a problem here—more than one because she refused to acknowledge what was happening. He couldn't be sure whether she was in denial or simply hiding the issue, but all the togetherness they were sharing on this vacation hadn't succeeded in getting her to open up.

"Come here, Miranda." He hoped she didn't recognize his raw tone for the disappointment it was.

Threading his fingers around her waist, he helped her maneuver until he could pull her into his arms. She stretched out, her legs twined with his, their bodies pressed close so he could feel her smooth curves against him.

With a few tugs, he loosed the blindfold until he

found himself staring into her sultry blue eyes, a gaze that could be polished and cool or so alive with pleasure. Her expression was shadowed now, unreadable, as if she shielded her thoughts behind an invisible wall. He thumbed her cheek, a touch he hoped conveyed his yearning, the pleasure he felt to be with her again.

"I love you, Miranda." He moved in for a kiss, and his mouth caught hers, his tongue sweeping inside to prove he meant what he said.

He loved her, for better or worse, *always*.

Miranda snuggled close and returned his kiss with a longing that might have surprised him if he'd missed what had just happened. But he felt her restlessness now, sensed her need for reassurance, even if he didn't know what she needed to be reassured about. He couldn't understand what was happening with her, why she'd gone from hot to cold, unless she talked to him. She wasn't and that bothered him. *A lot.*

When they finally broke their kiss, he leaned back against the chaise. "I just want to lie here and hold you for a while."

"Your wish is my command, Lieutenant Commander."

He *wished* she would tell him what was wrong. But he wasn't going to ask again. The last time he'd tried to get her talking, she'd only given him a bunch of evasions. Then she'd retreated behind her perfect wife persona—exactly what she was doing now.

She seemed blissfully unaware of anything but this chance to snuggle. Pressing her face against his shoulder, she let her eyes flutter closed and skimmed her lips along his throat, a natural, unconscious gesture that at any other time might have made him smile.

He wasn't smiling now, and as he held her, Troy considered his options. She'd been on edge ever since they'd started this vacation. He'd attributed her mood to logistics. Niagara Falls was her hometown, and a vacation to Falling Inn Bed meant close quarters with her estranged cousin, the woman hosting the Naughty Nuptials. Add that to watching her parents gear up for an election and dealing with the antics of her big-hearted, too-wild sister, and Troy thought he'd understood why she'd had them holing up inside the Egyptian Pleasure Pyramid instead of running all around town to visit with family and friends.

But Troy had been wrong.

Suddenly everything made sense. Miranda had been trying to reassure him that everything was okay, trying to distract him from what he knew in his gut—they were in trouble. But she'd plastered a smile on her face and pretended that everything was fine.

Like she'd just done while making love.

And when Troy thought about it, he couldn't remember the last time she'd initiated sex. He'd been doing the honors on this vacation. He couldn't remember back before his latest deployment. How long had this been going on?

He probably wouldn't like the answer, but he was glad she'd chosen distraction over faking an orgasm.

That would have hurt.

Burying his face in her curls, he inhaled deeply of her scent, so feminine and all Miranda. With only a week left of their holiday, he needed to reevaluate his game plan. Once they headed home, their lives would be full of commitment and routine. It would be all too easy for her to hide, and then he'd get orders and head out again.

He needed to get Miranda to share what was on her mind now, while they had only each other to focus on, so they could figure out what was happening and how to deal with it.

He wouldn't let this go on any longer.

She'd had her chance to fess up. He was done with evasions, done watching his wife retreat behind that persona she wore in public.

He wouldn't let her get away with it anymore. Confrontation would be a tactical error that would only put her on the defensive. No, he had to start pushing, but he had to push purposefully, quietly.

As if sensing his resolve, Miranda nestled closer and gave a small sigh, her mouth parting around the soft sound. She had a kissing mouth, a mouth that smiled with such dazzling perfection that he always wanted to tease her until she couldn't resist brushing those moist lips against him.

Her mouth had been the first thing he'd noticed about her. Miranda was the kind of beautiful that made men stupid. He vividly recalled how his fellow officers who had toured her college group through their naval base had made asses of themselves over her.

Troy might have gotten stupid, too, had it not been for her too-cool composure that had challenged him. He could still remember how her self-possessed smiles had dared him to make her laugh, or frown. He'd wondered what it would take to get her to let her hair down.

And make her sigh with pleasure.

Troy had sensed they were a pair. Two people with adventurous souls. He'd been raised without limits while Miranda had been taught to keep her sense of adventure reined tight. With her high-power family, she'd honed her public persona to a sharp edge, but beneath that composure beat a light heart. He'd wanted to be the man to help her discover that part of herself, and he'd always tried to be supportive.

But no more.

He wouldn't sit around and wait for Miranda to come clean. She'd had her chance. *Too* many chances. He wouldn't let her slip away without a fight.

He wouldn't let her slip away. Period.

MIRANDA HAD STARTED the morning off with high hopes of enjoying a relaxing day with Troy. No Naughty Nuptials events. No visits with family or friends.

She should have known better.

Crashing and burning on the way to an orgasm clearly wasn't enough to deal with this morning. Now a phone call from her sister pitched her day from bad to worse, and she was *this close* to declaring mutiny and abandoning ship on this whole vacation.

Settling the telephone back on the cradle, she cocked a hip against the desk and stared out into the courtyard, flooded with sunlight from the glass ceiling. What appeared to be a bright day in the Egyptian Pleasure Pyramid's oasis didn't feel anything but gloomy and dismal.

Troy emerged from the kitchen, carrying a plate. "Lunch. I made enough for us both."

His man-size sandwich surrounded by a mound of pickles and tortilla chips almost made her smile. "Thanks. But I'm not hungry just now." Her appetite had gone the way of her orgasm.

"So what's up with your sister?" He arranged his meal on the table.

"Victoria wants me to meet her in the photojournalist's room so she can talk to me. Laura Granger will be there."

"Laura, why?" He sounded surprised, and she wasn't sure why. They were dealing with her younger sister here, a woman who lived life to throw monkey wrenches in situations just to see what happened.

"She didn't say."

Meeting with the photojournalist wasn't a problem. But Laura Granger? Her estranged cousin was about the last person Miranda wanted to meet with any day—especially a day that had taken such a downhill turn. She was already scrambling not to let her vanishing orgasm spoil her mood.

Maybe Victoria could ignore the longtime rift between their family and Laura's. She was the only one, though. People in this town always paid close attention whenever Fords and Grangers came together, and personally, Miranda couldn't see what was so fascinating.

Their mothers were sisters. So what if Laura was the daughter of a rebel socialite who had abandoned her family to run off with an artist? That only proved Laura's mother cared more about herself than the needs of her family.

Good riddance, as far as Miranda was concerned.

"Well, I suppose it's to be expected," she said. "I knew I'd have to deal with the whole family issue when I let you talk me into getting married at Laura Granger's hotel."

She couldn't lament that choice now. If she hadn't

agreed to have the wedding here, then they'd never have been invited back as the Hottest Honeymoon Couple. She'd wanted a fantasy wedding and vacation. Now she would pay the price.

"You let me talk you into getting married here because you knew this place would be fun." Troy dropped a pickle back onto the plate, leaned back and shot her a sober look. "And you knew if you went along, I'd make it worth your while. I've held up my end of the deal."

That wasn't a question, and Miranda's heart sighed at the memory of the easier time in their lives and how well he'd held up his end of the deal. A wedding night in the exotic Roman Bagnio suite where they'd soaked naked in the baths. Three weeks touring the Hawaiian Islands where they'd made love on their own private beach during sunrises and sunsets.

He'd been living up to his end of the deal. No question.

"Perhaps the Naughty Nuptials wasn't such a great idea," she admitted. "Maybe we should have gone someplace where we didn't know anyone for our vacation."

"Done deal. Besides, we've been so busy with these events that you haven't had much time to spend with anyone but me. I'm surprised your family and friends haven't beaten down the door."

"Everyone knows we're here for the grand opening. And we deserve some time together."

"Agreed, but I expected to do some sharing. You haven't been home in six months. People want to see you."

"Like Victoria and Laura Granger," she said dryly. "I would assume this has something to do with Hottest Honeymoons, but if so, why would she only invite me? I wonder if this has something to do with her engagement."

"You sound skeptical."

"What else can I be, Troy? My sister's involved with Laura Granger and engaged to a man she just met. This is even more insane than her usual insanity."

"Could be worse. She could have run off to Vegas to live with Adam."

No argument there. But the whole situation was so classic Victoria that it was hard to be objective. "Who knows if that wedding will ever take place? They might decide they don't like each other once they become acquainted."

"Maybe, maybe not. They know they're in love. What more do they need to know?"

There was a soft quality to his voice, a sound that implied he'd be equally insane for her. Not so long ago that admission would have melted her heart, but now…*now* it reminded her she hadn't been living up to *her* end of the deal.

"I guess I should get this over with." She had better things to expend her energy on—like figuring out how to keep her worries out of the bedroom for the rest of their vacation.

"I'll come with you," Troy said.

She turned to find him leaving the table. "I appreciate it, but finish your lunch. I won't be long."

"I've been waiting four months to be with you. I don't want to waste more time if I can help it."

"I like when we're together."

"Me, too, Mrs. Knight. Me, too."

And as she watched him cross the room to return his

plate to the kitchen, she saw the determination in his long strides, knew he wanted to be with her because he recognized that she dreaded this visit.

That was Troy, solid, *there*. Even when they were physically apart, he tried to stay involved and supportive. She appreciated the effort. But lately that closeness let him sense she was off, despite her best efforts to reassure him.

She simply had to pull herself together so she could get on with the important things in life…like enjoying together time with her husband on a fantasy vacation that most couples only dreamed of.

Making her way into the bedroom, Miranda refreshed her makeup, and Troy soon followed, heading into the bathroom with the promise, "I'll take a fast shower."

"Fine." She glanced into the mirror where she found a stranger staring back.

Who was this woman who had let worry chase away *another* orgasm?

Miranda didn't know.

She'd always been a capable, accomplished woman who had no trouble achieving what she put her mind to. Public speaking. Spearheading a variety of volunteer fund-raisers. Graduating from college cum laude. Whenever she set a goal, she learned the skills necessary to accomplish the job then did it. No problem.

She'd fallen in love, gotten married and planned to be the perfect wife. She'd intended to accompany Troy on his tours, support his career and keep the home fires burning while he was on duty.

She'd understood the responsibilities involved, knew

what it would take to support a man with a power career, and was willing to do the job. She'd learned from the best—her mother handled the demanding role of politician's wife with grace and ease. Miranda had felt eager and ready for her future as Troy's wife.

It had never occurred to her that she couldn't transition her skills into military life.

But that's exactly what was happening.

Dropping the lipstick into her purse, she glanced down at the dresser where Troy's wallet sat neatly beside his watch and the suite's keycard. His organizational skills were a side effect of his upbringing, a tangible reminder of how different he was from any man she'd ever known.

If Miranda didn't love him so much, she might not feel so badly right now. But she did love him enough that she desperately needed to figure out how to deal with the situation *before* he found out life was exploding in her face back home.

The memory of her latest failure hit her fast and hard, and humiliation came as white-hot and excruciating as it had during her latest attempt to make a place for herself with the wives of Troy's peers. Closing her eyes, Miranda couldn't face herself in the mirror when she remembered taking her turn as hostess for their monthly tea.

I want the event to be special, she'd told the local florist. *So let's go with a springtime theme to celebrate April showers and May flowers.*

She remembered standing in the doorway of the clubhouse to survey the effect, found herself pleased with the result. Tables had been decorated with colorful floral arrangements, sparkling glassware and a variety of goodies catered by a well-known teahouse she'd heard many of the women rave over.

She wanted to make a good impression—the officers' wives were a tight network on this naval base, a support system through the steady rounds of "hails and farewells," bosses' nights and unaccompanied tours. Through them, she could learn the social dos and don'ts to help further Troy's career.

For some reason, her infiltration into their ranks hadn't been smooth, and she'd wanted this tea to bridge the distance. She remembered smiling while gazing around that beautifully decorated room.

And she'd still been smiling when she'd donated every last finger sandwich to a local ministry because none of her guests had shown up. Not one. The women had made their point that day—they wouldn't accept her no matter what she did to fit in.

Opening her eyes, Miranda forced herself to meet her reflection, to acknowledge that this hadn't been her first failure, though it definitely qualified as her most spectacular. She'd dubbed those women the witchy wives that day, and refused, absolutely *refused,* to let them make her life miserable. But despite that vow, she'd begun dreading the orders that took Troy away. When he left, she felt stranded across the country from friends and family.

And from Troy.

Even worse was that she couldn't discuss the problem with Troy. *Wouldn't* discuss it. Early in their marriage he'd made it clear he expected her to handle what came up while he was gone, trusted her to deal with their domestic life.

Funny, but she remembered that debacle almost as clearly as hosting the officers' wives tea.

Things had seemed pretty simple and straightforward at the time. Her car had needed some expensive repairs, and the dealer had recommended trading it in on a newer model rather than pouring money into hers. She agreed but had wanted Troy's input before signing off on a three-year loan.

She'd tried to contact him for several days via their usual lines of communications, but when she didn't hear back from him, she'd assumed he was out of touch on a mission. Since the situation hadn't been an emergency, she'd done the next best thing and sent him a telegram.

What she hadn't realized was that her telegram would be handled by *a lot* of people on its way to Troy.

Everyone from the telegram messenger and the chaplain to his unit commander and team members had learned the details of her transportation situation. Troy's response had been equally simple and straightforward— deal with it.

She'd never meant to embarrass him and had learned a valuable lesson. Her husband was in special operations and didn't need to be distracted with minutiae. Distractions risked a lot more than a disgruntled client or a lost account. Troy's life hung in the balance of his job performance, along with the lives of his teammates and their mission objectives.

If Troy had any idea how badly the situation had degenerated at home, he'd be worrying about her while trying to work. She refused to let that happen. Not for a bunch of witchy women who shouldn't be bothering her.

But they were. For some reason their rejection had

made her doubt herself. She should be above their petty rudeness, but she'd started questioning whether she was cut out for the military, if her upbringing and family name had paved her way by making life too easy.

She'd been a big fish in the little pond of Niagara Falls. She'd never considered the obstacles she might encounter as a little fish in a big pond. But she was facing them now.

And had vowed to overcome them.

She would keep the home fires burning so Troy could look forward to returning home to a wife who couldn't wait for him to get there. She would keep her worries out of their bed while on this fantasy vacation.

She just wished the job didn't feel quite so big.

3

MIRANDA WOULD SAY one thing—Laura Granger had created a fantasy with her Wedding Wing. As she and Troy headed toward the elevator to take them down to the third floor, she couldn't help but marvel at the grandeur of this new addition.

She would never have guessed the oddball girl who'd been a constant irritation during school would be responsible for breathing life back into this old hotel.

As Laura had always been the one lurking in the shadows, Miranda couldn't help but think how life had reversed their positions. Laura stood in the spotlight of her grand opening, while Miranda had come on this vacation to escape.

Slipping her fingers through Troy's, she took comfort in his touch and tried to shake this contemplative mood.

She was thinking again.

As always, Troy proved a great distraction. When the elevator deposited them on the third floor, he slipped his arm around her and pulled her close for a quick kiss before directing her to the room where the photojournalist had set up headquarters during the grand opening.

Miranda couldn't imagine what the man had cooked up with her sister and Laura Granger. Tyler Tripp might be acclaimed for his work, but he was also thoroughly disreputable looking, exactly the sort of more-tattoos-than-college-credits type of man her sister typically got involved with. Given their shared interest in journalism, Miranda couldn't believe Victoria had hooked up with ultraprofessional Adam Grant instead.

"All set?" Troy asked when they arrived at the room.

"Showtime."

He knocked. Taking a deep breath, Miranda steeled herself as the door opened, but to her surprise, Tyler wasn't anywhere to be seen. Only Victoria.

"Thanks for coming." Her sister resembled their mother in appearance with her bright red hair and fair skin, but the similarities ended there. Victoria's enthusiasm was all her own.

"Not a problem that I came, too, is it?" Troy asked.

Wrapping her arms around Troy's neck, Victoria gave him a hug. "Of course not. You're my favorite bro-in-law."

He was Victoria's only brother-in-law, as they all well knew, but Troy clearly appreciated the welcome. So did Miranda. She forced a smile.

Laura Granger waited inside, and she didn't look nearly as enthusiastic to see them. They'd grown up disliking each other. Laura was everything Miranda wasn't—tall and slim with white-blond hair, pale blue eyes and luminous skin. Given the way their families led separate lives, comparisons were inevitable. Given their differences, disliking those comparisons was also inevitable.

And people in their town were fascinated by a prominent family that had split down the middle. While Miranda had the benefit of hailing from the still respectable and affluent side of the family, Laura had suffered her family's fall from grace with not much to define her but her stunning looks and ambitious academic marks. She'd been out of her league with the other students at prestigious Westfalls Academy.

Add Victoria to the mix now, with her glorious hair and come-hither smiles, and it might explain why Miranda suddenly felt like the runt of the litter.

"Nice to see you both." With her smile firmly in place, Laura was in full hospitality management mode. "Thanks for meeting with us on your day off."

"So what's up?" Miranda directed her question to her sister, eager to get this ball rolling. The sooner they got to the point, the sooner she could deal with the fallout and get on with her day. And there would be fallout. After a lifetime of dealing with Victoria, she knew there was *always* fallout.

"I'm here to sell you on an idea, big sis." She gestured them to the sofa while heading toward the desk and Laura. "Sit. Would you like anything to drink?"

Shaking her head, Miranda sat beside Troy, who nudged his knee against hers as if to say, "This should be interesting."

No doubt. "Might I ask why you invited me to Tyler's room when he doesn't seem to be around? Is this about Hottest Honeymoons?"

"Not exactly," Victoria said. "We wanted neutral turf. When you came to the Wedding Knight Suite, I thought you were going to have a heart attack." She glanced back at Laura. "The rack. She thinks I'm a closet dominatrix."

Laura only inclined her head, but her amused expression irked Miranda. Yes, the pornographic sex device that comprised a *whole wall* in Victoria's suite had surprised her, but when had these two become such good friends that they discussed her?

Miranda refused to ask. What they did on their own time wasn't her concern—unless their actions started the town talking again. Her mother didn't need the stress right now. Not while dealing with Victoria's unexpected engagement.

"We could have used Laura's office," Victoria explained. "But I wasn't sure I could get you there. So we begged a favor from Tyler—" she swept an arm around to encompass the tastefully decorated guestroom "—and here we are."

"There's a method to our madness, too," Laura added. "What we want to show you is on Tyler's computer."

"Really? Now I'm curious."

"Me, too," Troy said. "Why don't you start the show?"

Laura sat down behind the desk and slanted the monitor toward them. She clicked the mouse to bring up an image of formally dressed guests in what could have been one of many grand opening functions that had taken place over the past two weeks.

"All right," Victoria said. "But give me a chance to explain everything before you blast our idea out of the water, would you, big sis?"

Our idea?

The thought of Victoria and Laura Granger colluding over anything was enough to send a cold chill up Miranda's spine. But she nodded, willing to agree to just about anything if her sister—who was dragging out the suspense as usual—would get a move on. "Why are you even making the effort if you're so sure I'm going to disapprove?"

"You know me. Hope springs eternal." Her sister gave a laugh, which transformed Laura's hospitality-perfect veneer into a worried frown.

Curiouser and curiouser. There was *a lot* going on between these two if she read the signals right.

Cocking a hip against the desk, Victoria folded her arms. "When I was first assigned to cover the Naughty Nuptials, I put all the family history on the table to get any questions of bias out of the way. This got me and Laura talking about what really happened to cause the trouble between her mother and Grandfather all those years ago."

That *trouble,* as Victoria called it, had caused their grandfather to disown his oldest daughter and had instigated a family rift that had lasted decades.

Leaning back against Troy, Miranda settled in for the long haul. Judging by her sister's excitement, she intended to play this for all it was worth.

"Got it," Miranda prompted. "So you two rehashed past history. I won't ask why."

"It's irrelevant, anyway. What is relevant is that we decided we needed to find out what really happened. So we've been talking to Aunt Suzanne and Mother."

Aunt Suzanne? When had Laura Granger's mother become *Aunt Suzanne?*

"I'll have you know that Mother was very forthcoming with me," Victoria continued. "Aunt Suzanne, too. And in getting both sides of the story, Laura and I learned that there are some really big questions about our family history."

"What sort of questions?" she asked.

"Like how come we were told our grandmother was English."

From the corner of her eye, Miranda caught sight of Troy's frown and supplied the reason. "Because she was English. Mother said she came to America from England after they married."

"She told me the same thing."

"So did my mom," Laura added.

"And you're saying she didn't?" These two had to be off their rockers. She couldn't vouch for *Aunt Suzanne,* but Miranda knew her mother would never mislead them about the parent she'd lost in a car accident while still a very young child.

"As far as they're concerned, our grandmother did come from England," Laura explained. "Tori and I haven't told them what we've found out yet."

"What's that?" Troy threaded his fingers through Miranda's, a silent show of support.

"Grandfather said he'd met our grandmother during the war and married her before they came back to the United States. Well, I've been doing some investigating and couldn't find a thing about his marriage to Laura Russell. I got curious, so I looked into her immigration records. If she was a British citizen, she had to have papers to get into this country."

Victoria met her gaze with an expression positively alive with excitement. "Laura Russell doesn't seem to have existed until she appeared in the good old U.S. of A, fully grown and married to our grandfather."

"I should add that Tori had to dig for this information." Laura gave a tight laugh. "I'm still waiting for Interpol to show up in the lobby."

"Pshaw." Her sister waved a dismissive hand. "Have a little faith, please. We're talking immigration here. I didn't have to dig *that* deep. Besides, I happen to be good at what I do. No problems, trust me."

Trusting Victoria was enough to strike terror in the bravest of souls, and Miranda was surprised Laura recognized it. "Exactly what did you learn? Our grandmother must have existed or the three of us wouldn't be here right now. Will you please tell us before you wind up in prison?"

"Oh, our grandmother existed, all right," Victoria said. "Only she wasn't English. She was a French citizen. Her name was Laure Roussell not Laura Russell."

Miranda wasn't at all sure what to make of this revelation, except that she could tell by her sister's expression that she was serious. "Victoria, that's crazy."

"I have documentation to prove it."

"Can you possibly be mistaken?"

"Not a chance. Grandfather's name is on the marriage certificate."

"And you don't think Mother knows?"

She shook her head and Laura agreed. "My mom, either. She named me after our grandmother. I'm Laura. No question there."

Troy looked as puzzled as Miranda felt. "If your information is accurate, then the question here would be *why*. Why would your grandmother hide her French ancestry? And why wouldn't the senator tell his daughters?"

"That's the mystery," Laura said. "And since we're pretty sure our moms don't know, we didn't want to start asking questions. Not until we have some idea of what this is about."

Miranda tried to digest this information. Their grandfather had been an Army commander during World War

II, had even been decorated after being captured by the enemy and leading many of his men in a daring escape.

She knew he rarely, if ever, discussed the war, and any media inquiries were always met with a stony "No comment." His handlers had spun his silence to make him look like a humble man who'd done his job and didn't feel comfortable with accolades.

"If Grandfather kept our grandmother's heritage a secret, then it must be a secret that needs to be kept," Miranda said. "Victoria, you know as well as I do that Grandfather would never sidestep this kind of information without good reason."

"I agree," Troy said. "The senator wouldn't risk the publicity if word ever leaked out. If you were able to uncover the information, no doubt other reporters could, too."

"Laura and I discussed that," Victoria said. "We believe everything looks nice and neat on the surface so no one will have any reason to dig into our grandmother's past. She died a long time ago. Before Grandfather became a senator."

"Let's hope it stays that way." Miranda meant it. "What if all this investigating raises unnecessary interest? You're a reporter. You know better than anyone how this could blow up in our faces. With Father up for reelection, the media would have a field day with this. And if Mother doesn't know…"

"It's a chance we'll have to take." Victoria's frown made the hair on the back of Miranda's neck prickle.

Laura nodded. "If we want to fix things."

"What do you want to fix?" Troy eyed them curiously as he slipped his arm around her.

"Our family," Victoria said. "We need to find out what happened so we can figure out how to solve the problem and bring our families back together again."

Why was Miranda even surprised? This was her sister they were talking about here, with Laura Granger tossed into the mix. A crazy combination no matter how she came at it. "What do you mean *fix* our family? What makes you think anyone wants to be fixed? I mean, if you two want to play nice, then have at it—"

"Not *us,* big sis."

Miranda barely got a chance to brace herself before Laura said, "Our mothers."

"They haven't talked for decades and seem content with the arrangement." She tried to sound reasonable, but didn't quite manage. These two had lost their minds. "What on earth makes you think that's likely to change?"

"Take a look at this." With a few maneuvers of the mouse and some blips and beeps, Laura enlarged the images on the computer monitor to reveal two familiar faces.

Miranda had honestly never realized how much her mother and Laura's looked alike. Her brief interactions with *Aunt Suzanne,* mostly at Westfalls Academy where the woman had once worked, had left Miranda with the memory of long dark hair and a wardrobe that favored comfort over style.

But while the woman wore long skirts and a minimum of makeup, a closer examination revealed Laura's mother to be as striking as Miranda's own.

The hair was different. The features were different, yet so much about the fine-boned face was the same…the soft full mouth…the deep blue eyes…the aching look that made her face seem raw.

And her own mother…Miranda barely recognized her anguish. She'd watched her mother conduct press conferences filled with rabid reporters and not flinch, but here her expression openly wore the weight of too many years.

"Guess what they were looking at," Laura said.

"Each other." Victoria's voice was soft, affected in a way Miranda had never heard her before. "Tyler caught them on film. Can anything be worth this sort of heartache?"

Miranda didn't know what to say. Seeing this only drove home how right she'd been to worry about her mother.

When Miranda had married, Troy had been stationed in Virginia, close enough for her to return home for frequent visits. But not long into their marriage, he'd received orders to the naval base in San Diego. She simply couldn't make it home as often, and her mother had lost an important part of her support system.

Miranda knew because she'd felt the loss, too.

Victoria was more concerned with her own life than she'd ever been with their family. And given their prominence around town, her mother simply didn't have many friends she could trust or confide in. Certainly not many who understood the stresses of her position in a political family.

But even more concerning was what could happen if the reason for their grandfather's secrecy turned out to be some scandal. Miranda disliked airing personal business in front of Laura Granger, but as Victoria had chosen to collude with the woman…

"Mother doesn't need this sort of stress right now.

Neither does Father. His opponents will be looking for anything they can find to crucify him with. Even some old mystery. If Mother wanted to talk to *Aunt Suzanne*, don't you think she'd pick up the phone and call her?"

Laura shook her head, her hospitality-perfect expression fading behind a thoughtful look. "I don't. I think our moms are behaving exactly like they've been expected to behave."

"As who's expecting them to behave?" Troy didn't give Miranda a chance to ask as he leaned in close.

"The senator," Laura said. "When he and my mom had it out all those years ago, he told her to choose between her family and my father. She made her choice, and he disowned her. They were very young and the situation was cut-and-dried. He expected my mom to stay away and Miranda and Tori's mom not have any contact. That's exactly what they've been doing."

Victoria finally lifted her gaze from the monitor where their mother's face stared back with that haunted expression. "I'm not convinced that's what *they* want. Look at Mother, Miranda. If this is really what she wanted, would she hurt like this after so many years?"

"You're not a mind-reader, Victoria. You can't know that's what's happening here."

"No, I can't," she agreed. "But I don't need to be inside her head to know she's lonely and sad. Isn't it worth at least a shot? With you living across the country, and me moving to Las Vegas, wouldn't you feel better knowing she has someone she cares about in her life again?"

Miranda wasn't sure what surprised her more—her sister's conviction or her insight into their mother's situation. She'd honestly thought Victoria didn't pay attention to what went on in their family. But looking at her sister now…well, she could see that Victoria cared.

Unfortunately caring didn't mean her sister would act in a fashion that wouldn't stir up talk about the family, and getting a Ford and a Granger together would stir up talk. "Do you think Grandfather will just smile and wish them well?"

"I don't know what Grandfather will do. But I'm willing to bet if this family bands together, Mother and Aunt Suzanne won't have to spend the rest of their lives pretending they don't want to see each other to please a selfish old man."

Her vehemence left Miranda momentarily speechless, giving Laura a chance to stand and circle the desk. "I don't want to see your family in an awkward position. But I think Tori's right about this. If we pull together, we can change things. We've all been acting how we were expected to act. You and I are living proof."

Troy squeezed her hand and she knew he was gauging her reaction, but she wouldn't give any of them a reaction.

Trying to bridge the rift between their families could only stir up trouble, and that's not what she wanted for her mother right now. This craziness would only wind up ticking off their grandfather once and for all, getting Victoria disowned, and then her mother would have to contend with splitting her loyalties between her father and daughter. And Miranda would be clear across the country and not much help.

"What are you talking about, Laura?" she asked. "We're proof of what?"

"I've been doing a lot of soul searching lately." Laura

sounded thoughtful. "When I think about our years at Westfalls, I realize I didn't dislike you because of who you were. I honestly never made an effort to know you. But I hated being compared to you and always coming out on the short end."

As much as Miranda hated to admit it, she could relate. Their families were as different as caviar and peanut butter, and being from the caviar side might have afforded her the benefits of wealth and privilege, but along with those benefits came some responsibilities. Public visibility and living up to the standards that generations before her had established were only two of them. Another was pleasing her grandfather.

She sensed Troy drinking this all in. Aside from an overview of family history, she'd never explained the details of her relationship with Laura Granger. As far as she was concerned, Laura was past history, but he couldn't miss there was more water under this bridge than he knew.

"What is it you want from Miranda?" he asked.

"This is the first time we're all together since Westfalls Academy," Victoria said earnestly. "The first time Mother and Aunt Suzanne have been in the same room in years. Come the end of the week, Naughty Nuptials will be over. We'll all go back to living our separate lives. We won't get this chance again, and if there's any way we can solve this problem, I think we should try. Since Miranda's a part of the family, she should be involved."

"What about talking to the senator?" he said. "Because Miranda's right, you don't want to raise any red flags with your investigation. Who knows what might crop up."

Victoria gave a huff of exasperation. "I agree with

you, bro-in-law, but do you honestly think he'll tell us what we want to know when he hasn't even told his daughters?"

In a normal family, Troy's suggestion would have been a good one. In the Knight family, simple communication would have done the trick. But Miranda didn't come from a normal family. Her grandfather was a very strong-willed, very stern man. In fact, she had a really hard time imagining any of them—for all their bravado—confronting him about secrets from his past.

Miranda met Troy's gaze and squeezed his hand to let him know how much she appreciated his efforts to run interference with these two schemers.

"Why don't we just talk to our respective mothers and encourage them to get together," she suggested. "If they want to, they will. If not, no harm no foul. They'll think we've all lost our minds, but no one will wind up in an awkward position. You're right in one regard, Laura. I don't really know you, but I assume you don't want this town to start gossiping about your parents again."

"Of course not," she said. "But I do think we need to put the past behind us if we can."

"You're looking for a miracle."

A slow, easy smile spread across her face. "It so happens that we specialize in miracles at Falling Inn Bed."

"Forgive me, Laura, but you specialize in sex," Miranda said, squelching her impatience. "You might pretty it up like you did in my suite, but I saw the dungeon Victoria's staying in."

Her sister laughed. "It was the rack. I told you."

Miranda only stared at the two of them, uncomfortable with being the object of their amusement.

"Ladies, would you mind explaining how you plan to avoid raising red flags?" Troy asked.

Victoria launched into a breathless account of how they would delve into their grandparents' lives, and if anyone got interested—which she was sure they wouldn't—then they'd just pretend to be tracing their genealogy.

As Miranda listened to her sister and Laura, she agreed their plan might yield the answers they were looking for without inviting any interest from the press. But she wasn't willing to take that chance. Not when they had no idea what they might find.

Before she had a chance to make her argument, though, Troy said, "I can help out with the records. It's going to be tough to find out about the senator's orders during his military career, but I've got some access. I should be able to get basic information."

For a space of a heartbeat, Miranda could only stare up at her husband.

He was *offering* to help?

She recognized his determination to assist in this plan, despite her attempts to convince these two otherwise.

"This is a family situation, Miranda," he said. "And I'm family. I don't mind helping if it will get us some answers without cluing anyone in to what we're doing."

She still couldn't manage anything more than a stare, so he leaned close and whispered for her alone, "Damage control."

"I knew there was a reason you were my favorite bro-in-law." Victoria launched forward to kiss his cheek. "You're hired. So what about you, big sis? Are you on board, too?"

All gazes turned to her, and it was then that she finally realized what was happening.

She was getting dragged into this madness whether she wanted to or not.

4

MIRANDA WILLED HERSELF to smile graciously as Laura suggested they meet in her suite later for dinner to officially begin their investigation.

"We'll make my room headquarters and discuss how best to proceed," she said.

"Good idea," Victoria agreed. "You'll like the Castaway Honeymoon Isle, Miranda. No perverted sex toys in there. It's tasteful, like your suite."

Right. Tasteful seemed sort of irrelevant when they were about to cross long-drawn lines with this scheme to bring the Fords and the Grangers together. All the nuances of the situation hadn't hit her yet, but they would as soon as she had a chance to think about what they were about to do. At the moment, the whole situation just felt strange.

Even her husband felt like a stranger. He'd leaped feetfirst into this investigation even as she tried to dissuade her sister from investigating. He must have thought he was helping, but it wouldn't be the first time he expected her to handle her family the way he would have handled his own.

But the Fords were nothing like the rambunctious Knights. The six Knight siblings always made holiday get-togethers feel like the inside of a hurricane tunnel. Her mother-in-law reveled in having family around and encouraged her children to have fun and make memories.

Miranda loved her in-laws, but she couldn't deny the activity level sometimes overwhelmed her. Those times she sought out her father-in-law, an admiral, who always seemed like the calm in the middle of a storm.

She couldn't deal with her family the same way she and Troy dealt with his, and most of the time, he understood that.

But how could she argue his point now?

Victoria plus Laura Granger equaled trouble and the situation required damage control. Like it or not. And yet…had Troy backed her up when it counted, she might have put a stop to this craziness.

After they said their goodbyes, she and Troy left the photojournalist's room, but once inside the elevator, she brushed his hand from the control panel and depressed the lobby button.

"We're not going back to our suite?" he asked.

"No, the spa."

"Why?"

"Because I feel the need for a relaxing soak in the whirlpool. Or the sauna, if you prefer." She needed to clear her head and make some sense of what had just happened.

Troy narrowed his gaze. "You're angry."

"I'm not angry."

"No?" He arched a brow, a skeptical look that at any other time might have earned a smile from her. His striking green eyes contrasted sharply with his blond hair and tanned skin, making even a glance potent. "If you're not angry, what are you?"

Miranda considered her answer as the elevator came to a stop and unloaded them in the Wedding Wing lobby, in full view of the Mireille Marceaux painting showcased in a display. "I'm amazed Laura managed the loan of this painting from Westfalls."

He frowned.

"I'm not discussing your defection here in the lobby, Troy." She wouldn't discuss it at all until she'd had a chance to gather her thoughts.

"My *defection?*"

She ignored him and looked up at *The Falling Woman.* The stunning redhead and the surrounding forest gleamed in mist from the falls. The sheer veil she draped over her body poured over her like a waterfall, enhancing rather than covering the curves below. Miranda could make out a hint of blush-colored nipples, the triangle of glossy hair between her thighs.

"Laura told us her mother pulled some strings to arrange the loan," Troy finally said. "Since her mother worked at your school, I don't see what's so amazing."

"Laura's shown considerable business savvy by using this painting to generate local interest in her grand opening."

Troy led her across the lobby, staring up at the painting as if he couldn't figure out what the fuss was all about. "Because of the mystery surrounding the artist?"

"Her mystery has become legend around here."

A French painter from the middle of the last century, Mireille Marceaux had been known for her erotic oil paintings and sketches, although posthumously her landscapes had earned renown as well. After her unexpected death, she'd bequeathed the bulk of her estate to Westfalls Academy. The legend involved her mysterious connection to the academy and the Niagara Falls area.

"*The Falling Woman* is erotic art," Miranda explained. "When my mother was in school, Westfalls administration wouldn't acknowledge the existence of anything but the landscapes."

"Understandable for the time. But I don't think this painting is considered too risqué by today's standards."

"I suppose that's what makes her erotic—she leaves room for the imagination. When I remember how the students speculated about her art when I was in school... We expected pornography, but there's nothing pornographic about her."

With her face partially obscured in shadow and mist, *The Falling Woman* looked ethereal, almost mysterious. Miranda hadn't taken the time to look closely at her before, but after so recently examining the images of her mother and *Aunt Suzanne,* she noticed this woman's thoughtful expression, as if she'd known people would look at her and wonder what she was thinking.

Miranda didn't know if someone had modeled for the artist. Laura Granger would likely have that answer, *if* she wanted to ask the question. She didn't.

"So what do you think the artist's connection is?" Troy asked, tucking her closer against him, a natural move that sent a little tingle through her and went a long way to distract her from this portrait.

"I think Mireille Marceaux's name became so famous that she hid out here to be far away from the press and her critics."

"Laura mentioned during one of the receptions that people think a married man or an illegitimate child factored into the equation."

Miranda shrugged. "No one knows what Mireille Marceaux looked like, so it could be, I suppose. But if a mysterious artist left loved ones behind, I think someone would have surfaced by now to document her story, or write a tell-all book."

Troy glanced down at her with a searching expression. "That's an entirely different spin from Victoria and Laura."

"I'm not Victoria or Laura." And she had an entirely different spin on what it was like to be caught in the public eye. Who could blame this artist for keeping her identity hidden. Smart woman.

"No, you're you." Troy gave a laugh and pressed a kiss to the top of her head. "Have I told you lately I'm glad you're exactly who you are?"

"No, but I know you are anyway."

That certainty was a feeling she needed to cherish, she reminded herself. The most wonderful man in the world loved her. She shouldn't let a bunch of self-doubt about witchy wives and vanishing orgasms make her forget.

She just needed to focus on what was important right now—enjoying this precious time together with Troy.

"So what'll it be?" she asked as they turned the corner leading to the spa. "The whirlpool or the sauna?"

"Sauna."

"The sauna it is then. Hot, naked skin works for me."

"Does it?" He slanted a questioning gaze down at her.

"I didn't think you'd trust me again so soon after this morning."

"I always trust you, Lieutenant Commander. Before or after sex toys. Even cold ones. And after your dual-temperature torture device, it's *my* turn to pick the sex game…" She let her declaration trail off suggestively, and Troy flashed her a wicked grin.

Their arrival in the spa precluded more conversation, but there was no missing Troy's look of expectant male. Miranda smiled as they passed through the doors, feeling more in control than she had in too long. She wouldn't sacrifice any more time with her husband. Not to worry about Victoria and Laura. Not to worry about the possibility of vanishing orgasms.

"Good afternoon," a uniformed attendant greeted them, and they'd barely issued their request before being ushered to a private sauna and provided warm robes and towels.

She followed Troy's gaze around the dimly lit changing room decorated in an art deco theme. Stylized lamps glowed against tiled walls that were lined with bright hooks to hang clothing. A chaise and chair made of some slick fabric would hold up well to humidity.

As Troy drew near, she couldn't help wonder what he would think about her new game, knew she wouldn't have to wait long to find out. Not when he eyed her with a smile playing around his mouth, a look that said, "I've got you right where I want you."

This was a look she knew well, one that never failed to start her pulse racing. It was a look that chased away all other thoughts except for those of pleasuring and being pleasured by her husband.

"May I?" She trailed her fingers along his cheek and

down his neck, a searching touch that heightened the promise of the moment. Especially when she caught a glimpse of the jumping pulse in his throat.

"I'm all yours."

And the thought alone sent a sprinkling of sensation through her, heightened her excitement to begin her game. Slipping her finger into his collar, she caressed the pulse beat beneath his skin. The corners of his mouth kicked up in a smile as he shifted his gaze over her and appreciation flared in his eyes.

"I want you to know I will *not* be making love in this sauna, Lieutenant Commander." She unbuttoned his collar then continued down, exposing his tanned chest beneath his shirt.

"Really?"

She could hear the curiosity in his voice, didn't glance up. "*Really.* I've got a better idea."

He chuckled, a deep warm sound so close to her ear. "Better than making love? And what's that?"

"You'll see."

"If you don't want to make love, then why are you undressing me?"

"Can't resist." She brushed a kiss against his neck to sample the familiar taste of him. Then she leaned back and let her gaze drift down, down, *down*…and treated Troy to the sight of her skimming her hand along her stomach, dipping her fingers between her thighs, hinting at how warm and wet she'd gotten beneath her sundress. "Trust me, Lieutenant Commander. Turnabout is fair play and all that."

"And you trusted me this morning, hmm?" His voice had grown rough and all male.

"Blindfolded, too."

He was the only one showing skin right now, so she reached out to run her hands over his chest, to trace her fingers into each hollow and ridge. She liked the way his stomach contracted and the way he closed his eyes as if savoring the sensation. She liked switching the balance of power to make Troy react, to know he could get as wrapped up in pleasure as she could.

"But if we're not going to make love, Mrs. Knight, then this is nothing but torture—"

"Torture? Interesting word choice." Unfastening his belt, she went to work peeling away his pants and freeing a promising erection. Brushing her fingers over that hot length, she smiled when Troy sucked in a deep breath and swelled even more. "Is this really torture?"

Sinking to her knees, she decided she didn't have to be naked to *torture* him. Grazing her breasts against his thighs on the way down, she thrilled when his muscles trembled while she worked the jumble of clothing down his legs.

"Only if you leave me hanging."

Tipping her face up, she caught a glimpse of tanned skin and shifting muscle before she ran her open mouth along the underside of his erection. He swayed before steadying himself with a hand on the tiled wall.

"Hanging?" she demanded in a sultry voice. "Everything's at attention where I am."

Troy gave a throaty laugh that made his attentive *parts* jump in a sort of mock salute.

"Is this payback for the ice or because I got us involved with your sister and Laura?"

She shook her head, this time dragging her unbound

hair against him until his parts tangled in her curls. "Neither. It's just a game I want to play. I read about it in our introductory packet for the Naughty Nuptials. You remember. *A Lifetime of Desire: Couples Sensual Fantasies.*"

Troy groaned as she moved away, making his erection bounce again when it pulled free of her hair.

The sensual fantasies brochure had only been one of several that Laura had provided upon their arrival. After their long separation, she and Troy had gravitated toward the more obvious sex toys and games. But she'd remembered a game that would be perfect to buy her the time she needed to make it through the rest of their vacation.

Vanishing orgasms were simply unacceptable.

"Your dual-temperature torture device gave me the idea this morning. There's a game inside that fantasy brochure called Tease and Torture. I want to play that."

The *perfect* game.

He gave a grunt of laughter. "I knew torture factored in somewhere."

"It'll be good torture."

"*Good* torture? There's no such beast."

"Trust me." After setting aside his clothes on a chair, she returned to kiss the frown from his face. She shimmied close to his naked body in the process, unable to resist the lure of all those hard muscles. "We do whatever feels good, but we don't make love. We let the tension build."

"For how long?"

"Until I decide the game is over."

"And how long will that be? A day, a week, a month?"

"I don't know…*a while*. I want to give this a try to see how it goes. It'll be fun. And interesting. Think about it, Troy. Whenever you come home, we jump right in where we left off. We've been making love since we got here, so why not try something different? We've got all this time to ourselves. Let's see how long we can last without making love."

He eyed her closely, and she could see the gleam of interest deep in those crystal green eyes.

She forced a light laugh, hoping he didn't see how much she needed to play this game. "Don't you trust me?"

"I do. But I don't like playing games I know I'll lose." Before she realized what he was about, he'd snagged his arm around her and dragged her against him.

Gasping, she glanced into his face, where the dim light threw his strong features into backlight and shadow.

"There is no losing. We just keep building the tension. Eventually we'll make love. It's a win-win game."

"Until you decide it's over."

She nodded, nearly holding her breath as he eyed her with that clear gaze that saw too much.

"This is payback."

"It's not."

Troy couldn't know just how honest she was being. This wasn't about him at all. It was about not wasting their precious time together. About her learning to cope with a difficult situation. About not allowing doubt to hide under her pillow when she lay her head down to sleep.

And most of all it was about taking away the pressure so anxiety didn't chase her orgasms away.

He reached out to brush back strands of hair from her

temple, a thoughtful touch. "You're sure you're not angry?"

"I'm not. Honestly."

That sharp green gaze seemed to see inside her, but she could tell the instant he'd decided to play along because he inclined his head, obviously willing to take her at her word. "Then let's get you undressed for a little Tease and Torture."

"You'll play by the rules?"

"It works both ways, right? I get to torture you as much as you torture me?"

She nodded.

"Then your wish is my command."

Something inside her gave a huge sigh of relief and her only reply was a melting *"Mmm"* as he reached for the fastening of her sundress.

Gathering her hair, she piled it on top of her head to give him better access, shivering when he pressed an openmouthed kiss to her neck. His fingers danced against her skin as he unfastened the hook and eye then parted the collar.

Guiding her with his hands, he helped her manage her hair and free her arms. His breaths warmed her skin in sultry bursts as he trailed those kisses over her bare shoulder.

He raked his gaze down the length of her, and she watched a smile lift the corners of his mouth, appreciation flare in his eyes.

She felt so beautiful when he looked at her, and it was a potent feeling, one that had always amazed her. She hadn't known the feeling could disconcert her, too. But it could. When she'd been uncertain after the morning's debacle, that tender appreciation in his eyes, that love, had felt overwhelming.

But she tucked away those thoughts for later. Now wasn't the time for thinking about anything except this sensual moment. She didn't have to worry about intruding thoughts chasing away her orgasms now. This time was for exploring and enjoying and giving her attention to her handsome husband, who was reaching for the clasp of her bra and popping it open. Her breasts tumbled free, and he caught a nipple and squeezed, making her gasp.

Then he helped himself to the other.

Shrugging the bra down her arms, she let it slide to the floor, not wanting him to stop the touches that were making her breasts swell with pleasure and her nipples tighten.

And when he lowered his face…his moist mouth parted over her sensitive skin, a simple touch that forced another gasp from her lips, sent pleasure spiraling through her until she swayed on weak knees.

He flicked his tongue over a greedy peak, and his laughter burst against her skin, an erotic combination of warm breath and sound. "I'd like a painting of you wearing nothing but hair and mist. A small one, so I can keep it in my pocket when we're apart."

She thought of *The Falling Woman,* of the model who might have posed for the artist. The idea of standing naked to be sketched seemed daring in the extreme, titillating.

"Do you forget what I look like when you're away?"

"Hardly." Hooking his thumbs into the waistband of her hose, he tugged them down, leaving Miranda staring at the top of his head when he sank to his knees before her, slipping off her shoes and removing the hose with perfunctory motions.

He planted a kiss on her ankle. "I remember every inch of you. I want a painting so I can see you looking back with that wanting expression on your face."

Everything inside her seemed to dissolve as she imagined herself posing for that portrait. "Imagine what would happen if you lost it."

"You're so gorgeous you'd wind up displayed on some wall like *The Falling Woman*." Tipping his head back, he ran those piercing green eyes along every inch of her. "But I'd never let it out of my sight."

Not intentionally, she knew, but what if he was hurt on a mission? Just the thought made her throat constrict.

She was thinking again.

Urging Troy to his feet, she distracted herself by returning the favor. She would *not* let racing thoughts chase away her pleasure again.

She felt more relaxed than she had in a long time when Troy finally scooped her into his arms. His name left her lips on a laugh, and he shouldered open the door leading to the sauna.

"Grab some towels." He paused in front of a shelf while she grabbed a stack, and then stepped inside.

The hot, humid air made her suck in a tight breath. When Troy released her she took advantage of the moment by sliding down his body in a long, fluid motion that brought every sensitive inch of her into quick contact with him.

He groaned.

She gave a very deliberate laugh.

And by the time they were stretching out on the

benches inside the shadowy sauna—Miranda prone on the top bench so she could reach Troy supine on the shelf below—the warmth had seeped into her skin and made her feel bold.

Dangling her hand over the side, she brushed her fingertips lightly over his stomach until his muscles contracted and his erection bobbled. She gave it a stroke, too.

"Then how do you feel about helping out Victoria and Laura?"

"I'm not angry." How could she be angry about anything when she'd finally figured out how to fight back against her worries?

"So you keep saying." Slipping his arms behind his head, he stretched out more. "Then how do you feel—besides amazed Laura arranged the loan of *The Falling Woman?*"

She chuckled, liking this vantage with him spread out all tanned and naked and gorgeous beneath her. She couldn't resist skimming her hand into that smooth skin between his thighs, eliciting another bobble. "I'm trying to convince myself you're right and damage control is the best way to deal with Victoria."

"Do you really think you could have talked her and Laura out of investigating?"

"Maybe with some backup. I don't know how you could have missed that I didn't want to help them."

She ran her fingers between his thighs, cupping the velvet weight of his scrotum in her palm, watching his chest rise sharply when he sucked in a hard breath.

"I didn't miss it," he said. "But you weren't getting anywhere, so it made sense to move on to plan B."

"Is this some military strategy?"

"Split-second decisions are all in a day's work." He reached down to pick up where she left off stroking his erection, slow, easy strokes that were arousing her by the sheer eroticism of the sight. "Your sister's interested in why your grandmother changed her name. You don't understand that?"

"I don't understand why she was looking in the first place. Fixing this family will take more than a miracle."

Troy didn't argue, he just closed his eyes and kept up those lazy strokes. She gave another gentle squeeze and watched as goose bumps sprinkled along his skin.

"Don't get me wrong, Troy. If my mother wants to get together with her sister again, I'll support her a hundred percent. Even if it means making nice with Laura on holidays."

Those words scraped over her tongue, but Miranda meant what she said. She could handle Laura to make her mother happy.

"So you're not interested in finding out about your grandmother?" he asked.

"Whether I want to or not isn't the point. Avoiding potential fallout is."

His hand slowed its erotic rhythm, and he opened his eyes, staring up at her with a searching expression. "You'll sacrifice what you want to protect the family."

"Of course, but I don't consider this much of a sacrifice. I'd rather not know than live with potentially unpleasant consequences of whatever we might find out."

"You can't know the consequences will be unpleasant."

"My grandfather isn't stupid. He's held his own with politicians and the media for more decades than you and I have been alive. If he thought a name change needed to happen before he brought my grandmother to this country, I don't doubt it did."

"Victoria thinks he's being selfish."

"I can't say. But selfish or not, my grandfather doesn't act without a reason. She might know that if she paid more attention to what's happening in our family."

Miranda didn't want to talk about Victoria. Her sister had made the choice to play black sheep, and she suspected Victoria would keep making that choice until she got tossed out of the family like their aunt had.

She couldn't perform damage control for her sister, but she could make sure Victoria didn't land them in a situation they'd all regret.

"What do you think about me talking to Grandfather?" She dragged her hand along his thigh.

"More damage control?" Troy had started to sweat, and her hand glossed easily over his skin. She ran her palm over his hip and along that juncture between groin and thigh, pleased when he let out a breath that stuttered through the quiet.

Slipping her fingers back along his erection, she gave it a firm stroke that made his hips arch into her hands. "If there's a skeleton, I'd feel much better knowing it's not going to pop out when no one expects it."

"You're worried about your mother."

Miranda just nodded, pleased when he slipped his fingers around hers and speeded up her rhythm until his eyes drifted shut again. His whole body gathered, but he didn't slow their pace. "Will you tell him Victoria and Laura want to get your mothers together?"

"And risk giving him a heart attack? If our mothers

want to fix things, I think we'd all do well to let them handle Grandfather."

"Smart as well as gorgeous."

The words sounded as if he'd forced them out over broken glass, and she wasn't surprised when he removed her hand and rolled to prop himself up on an elbow.

Suddenly he could reach her and trailed his fingers between her thighs, a glancing touch that made her shiver despite the heat.

"I hope the senator comes clean so you can sidestep an investigation," he said. "I also don't think it's a bad thing to spend some time with your sister while we're home."

"And Laura Granger?"

"I'll reserve judgment. Lots of history you haven't shared." His fingers speared into the hairs she kept neatly trimmed over her sex, and she shivered again. "Las Vegas isn't that far from San Diego. I'd like to know you have some family close by when I'm away."

"Spoken like a man who's close to his siblings." She chuckled. "Might I point out that you have *normal* siblings?"

Troy caught a thatch of silky hairs between his fingers and gave a light tug that separated the sensitive folds below and made her sex clench in eager reply.

"You call Kevin normal? My brother sleeps all day, works all night and jets around town in a Porsche that cost more than his house."

"Your brother is a chef, silly man. When do you expect him to work if not at night?"

Sliding a finger toward that tiny knot of nerve endings, he zeroed in on the target with a steady rolling motion that started up an ache deep inside. "What about

Marietta? She's so busy jet-setting around the world that she'll never settle down."

"Leave Marietta alone. There's not a thing wrong with her vacationing with her friends. She works hard. She deserves to have fun."

"Mrs. Knight, the point is that I'm involved enough with my siblings to know what's going on in their lives."

"My mother keeps me current with Victoria—" At the look of sudden smugness on Troy's face, she knew she'd lost this argument. "So I'm not as close with my sister. That's just the way it is, Troy. I've got my parents and my friends, so don't worry about me."

Unfortunately those parents and friends were clear across the country where she'd left them, and she was making zero progress in establishing new relationships. But that was need-to-know information Troy didn't need to know.

Especially when he busily slid that greedy finger through her body's moisture, separating her skin and winning a definite reaction when her sex clenched again. "Are you trying to change my mind about when to end our game?"

"Will you change your mind?"

"Not a chance." And Miranda **meant it.**

5

TROY THOUGHT ABOUT joining Miranda in the shower as she prepared to meet her sister and Laura tonight. As impressive as the suite itself, the bathroom in the Egyptian Pleasure Pyramid housed a spa large enough for a couple to play in and a shower with a dozen wall jets.

But he'd booted the computer instead, telling Miranda he'd wanted this time to look at what historical information about the senator he could easily obtain. That had been his intention when he'd sat down. At least until he'd read the same article twice and still couldn't remember what it had said.

Then Troy found himself idly surfing their private Web site, searching for clues to what was happening with his wife at home.

As a wedding gift, his mother had given them a copy of the *Spouse's Guide to Surviving a Deployment*. He'd laughed at the gift, but Miranda had insisted they read the book together and implement many of the suggestions that would help them feel close during his long wartime deployments.

She'd placed his pictures around the house. He'd gotten into the habit of jetting off e-mail posts to keep her up on what was happening with work. He wrote letters longhand when he didn't have access to a computer, and mailed them in batches when he got back to civilization.

Miranda had learned HTML to construct a password-protected Web site, a virtual world where he could go whenever he needed a glimpse of home. Knights Online, she'd named it, an inviting place made up of photos from places they'd visited together. She rotated those photos regularly, so he could log on one day to find Niagara Falls. Another day a beach in Hawaii. Or the shore at Norfolk. The boardwalk in Atlantic City. The base in Nebraska, where his parents were currently stationed.

She had pages devoted to news about their families, and memories of their wedding and honeymoon. She'd even created a virtual tour of their house in San Diego that he could access whenever and wherever he could manage online access.

Troy didn't know a damn thing about HTML or Flash or whatever she used to create these pages, but he was impressed with her skill, and always grateful. He couldn't count the times during the past year and a half that he'd dragged in from a mission dog-tired, only to log on and find a chatty message from her, filling him in on news from the home front.

And how much she missed him. Always that.

She'd set up a chat room where they met whenever his schedule permitted and a bulletin board where they could post messages around the clock. This bulletin board saw more use because his orders happened 24/7.

He found himself skimming through the photos of their last visit to his parents' home at Thanksgiving. Miranda and his mother standing over the stove as they sampled stuffing from the turkey. Miranda and Marietta setting the table. She'd been laughing in that one, no doubt at something his high-spirited sister had said, and he was struck by how happy she looked.

Or was her smile simply the one she wore for the world, the one that hid everything she felt inside?

Tease and Torture. Another time he might have enjoyed the erotic potential of her game, but after this morning, he saw the game as just another way for her to withdraw. She was putting controls in a place where they'd never had any distance before—in bed.

Why?

Only Miranda could answer that question, but she wasn't sharing. And he wasn't waiting. Not anymore. Victoria and Laura's investigation had given him an opportunity to drag her out from behind that perfect persona she wore for the world.

He'd hoped they didn't find any long-buried skeletons that would embarrass her family, but the bottom line…Troy didn't care. Investigating the family secrets with her sister afforded him a chance to force Miranda into a new situation, and it was a chance he wouldn't pass up.

His next step would be to gather information. Staring at the computer monitor, he surfed page after page of the site, reading the captions on photos, paying close attention to every snippet of text she'd written, every bit of news she'd reported. He had a damn puzzle to put together here, and the perfect place to search for some pieces.

MIRANDA TOOK A DEEP breath and prepared to deal rationally with this crazy investigation, and by the time

Laura Granger's fiancé opened the door of the Castaway Honeymoon Isle, she had her smile fixed firmly in place.

"Come on in." Dale Emerson greeted them as they made their way inside the suite.

"Should prove interesting," Troy said.

"No doubt about it." Dale laughed. "I'm glad everything worked out and you could make it tonight."

While Miranda didn't agree with Dale's interpretation of *working out,* she didn't fault the man. Since the start of the grand opening, she'd found Dale to be thoroughly respectable, and very likable, which had come as somewhat of a surprise.

She'd never given any thought to the type of man Laura Granger might involve herself with, but somehow the Wedding Wing's architect wasn't what she'd expected. An attractive man—if one cared for dark-haired men—Dale had always been cordial, and if the fact that these two had been attached at the hip through every grand opening event was any indication, he seemed genuinely smitten with his new fiancée.

Personally Miranda preferred a man who understood the fine line between attentiveness and clingy. She and Troy might be apart often, but they didn't hang all over each other when they were together.

I've been waiting four months to get home to be with you, Troy had said earlier. *I don't want to waste more time apart if I can help it.*

Okay, well maybe they did cling, a little.

"Hello." Laura, looking casually elegant in a skirt ensemble, emerged from the kitchen to join them. With her pale hair hanging loose down her back, Miranda couldn't help but notice how she'd not only grown into her model-thin body, but had learned to showcase it to advantage.

"We're almost all set," she said. "Bruno sent up dinner, which I promise will be delicious, and Dougray's on his way up with some extra computer equipment I've requested."

With a smile, she motioned around the room. "Please, make yourselves comfortable. I had a buffet set up so we can all sit around and talk while we eat. We'll be ready to go as soon as Victoria and Adam get here."

Leave it to her sister to arrange a get-together then arrive late. Only *fashionably* late, Miranda hoped, because she didn't want to be stuck chitchatting with Laura and Dale.

"Mind if we take a look around?" she asked, looking for an escape.

"Please do. This suite caters to the stranded-together-on-a-desert-island fantasy." Laura waved them into the living room, and Miranda couldn't miss the way her new engagement ring sparkled beneath the light.

During the first week of the grand opening, Laura had insisted she and Dale were only dating. Then as if by magic—or a *miracle*—she sported a rock on her finger the size of Horseshoe Falls.

After her sister and Adam's spontaneous engagement... Well, Miranda hoped that whatever miracles were happening around this place would cover them when they started digging into their family's past.

When Troy let out a low whistle, Miranda followed his gaze to the wall of glass and the tropical paradise beyond.

"Wow," was all she could say at the sight before them. She'd been impressed by the oasis in the Egyptian Pleasure Pyramid, but this rushing waterfall and lush pool paradise was nothing short of awesome.

"Wow is right." Troy was already pulling her through the open doors. "Come on, Miranda. Let's check this out."

"Have fun. You can get into the bedroom and master bath from out there," Laura said before heading back to the kitchen.

"Almost makes me wish we'd been the featured wedding couple for the grand opening." Troy circled the pool, heading toward the waterfall, where a rocklike shelf had been built into the poolside, surrounded by blooming tropical plants. "This waterfall is six feet tall."

"Our wedding was lovely." And a lot less hectic, Miranda thought, remembering all of the functions they'd attended during the past weeks of the Naughty Nuptials. "And we had fun in the Roman Bagnio baths."

He smiled absently. "I'm not complaining. Just impressed with what Laura and Dale have done with this place."

She hadn't meant to sound critical. But being around Laura had always had the ability to put Miranda on edge. She would have thought that with so many years passing since Westfalls… Old habits died hard, apparently.

She'd hoped to avoid memory lane on this visit. Laura had steered clear of her while she and Troy had planned their wedding, assigning the job to an assistant. She'd expected similar treatment this time around.

Had it not been for Victoria, she might have had it, too.

But in all fairness, Laura had made a valid point when she'd said they'd never really known each other during school. Miranda had certainly never put forth any effort to know Laura, had never felt the need. But after living with a bunch of witchy women who were judging her unfairly, she had a different perspective.

"This suite is impressive." Joining Troy, she took his hand, and they stood together in the water-soaked quiet.

Similar to the layout of their suite, the Castaway Honeymoon Isle had been designed around the lagoon. The bedroom doors were thrown wide and they strolled inside, admiring the colorful Key West theme and the huge bed beneath the skylights. The bath also resembled theirs with a garden tub and shower with wall jets. The rush of running water pervaded the entire suite.

Troy snagged her for a kiss inside the bathroom, and Miranda melted into his arms, seizing the moment.

"Horny, Lieutenant Commander?"

"You have to ask after the way you worked me over in the sauna?" He ground his hips against her, letting her feel the solid bulge that only needed permission to become an erection.

"Guess not," she whispered against his mouth. "If it's any consolation, you're not the only one."

"Glad to hear it. I'd say my game's working." One kiss and she felt flushed and achy, her body reawakening with lightning speed.

He chuckled, a burst of warm breath against her lips. "I bet you never imagined you'd be making out in your cousin's bathroom."

"Not in a million years. But I like touching you."

"I like you touching me, too." And to prove his point, he dragged his tongue over her lower lip just as voices cued them in to her sister's arrival.

Miranda stepped out of his arms and gave a shaky laugh. "Looks like we'll have to pick this back up later."

Troy pressed his hand to his crotch and smoothed the bulge there. "Okay, ready."

They headed into the living room. One look at Victoria with her new fiancé, and Miranda realized that seeing these two together would take some getting used to. Adam Grant was exactly the kind of professional powerhouse Victoria had always run from, a man who, remarkably, reminded her a lot of Troy.

Her husband wore command with ease, and over the past two weeks, she'd found Adam no different. An attractive man with dark hair and eyes, he wore custom-tailored suits rather than a uniform. Despite the insanity of their hasty engagement, he appeared to have a calming effect on her sister. Or so Miranda hoped. It would be an unexpected perk in an otherwise crazy situation.

After exchanging greetings, they all sat around the suite, plates propped on laps or chair arms to enjoy a delicious feast from the hotel restaurant.

As usual, Victoria placed herself front and center. "Look at this—we're all a big happy family. Who'd have ever guessed?"

Not Miranda for sure.

"Let's recap so everyone has the details, and then discuss what we need to do."

Both her self-appointment to the role of leader and her suggestion met with polite agreement, and she recapped the details of their earlier conversation for the benefit of Adam and Dale, who, judging by the attention they paid their plates, had already heard the finer points.

"Basically we need to know three things," Adam said. "Who your grandmother really was, where the senator met her and why they changed her name."

Miranda liked the way the man boiled things down to the relevant issues. Apparently so did her sister, who smiled up at him in beaming approval. It was a totally non-Victoria look, a look that seemed almost intimate, and, well…*loving*.

This was going to take *a lot* of getting used to.

"Tracking down Laure Roussell and her family should be a matter of searching Internet databases and genealogy sites." Laura raised her hand to signal everyone's attention. "Since Dale and I don't have any specialized areas of expertise with investigating, we can handle that."

"Miranda and I are the logical choice to look into where the senator and your grandmother met," Troy said. "Like I said earlier, I've got access to certain military databases, so I can look into the senator's career and see where he was stationed. I'll need dates, though."

"Got them." Victoria reached down beside the sofa to retrieve her briefcase. "Or at least a time frame. I've got two marriage certificates with Grandfather's signature and I can't be sure which is accurate."

When Troy nodded, Adam said, "Which leaves Tori and me to figure out what the deal is with the name change."

"Our grandmother came into this country as Laura Russell, so her papers had to come from somewhere."

Miranda set her plate on an end table and leaned close to Troy as he perused the documents Victoria handed him.

"The U.S. didn't get involved in the war until after Pearl Harbor. Will you be able to find out when Grandfather was deployed?"

"I should," he said. "I'll *need* to get a clue where they might have met."

"One marriage certificate says they married in England after the war was over," Laura pointed out. "The other says before in France. How hard do you think this will be to find out which is right?"

Troy shrugged. "The war is well documented, so I'll have plenty of places to look for information."

"This all begins and ends with the senator," Adam said. "Tori was telling me how little she knew about the details of the senator's Army career—"

"All I'd ever heard mentioned was Grandfather being involved in some sort of transportation bombing that wound up getting him and his men captured in occupied France," Victoria said. "While I was working today, Adam researched media coverage from when Grandfather escaped the concentration camp."

Miranda didn't know much more about their grandfather's career than Victoria. He'd been injured in the concentration camp, and still walked with a cane to this day.

"I downloaded what I found," Adam said.

"Here, take a look." Propping her laptop on the coffee table, Victoria booted her system then spun the monitor around, manipulating through windows of news items about their grandfather's escape.

"It appears he was involved with preparation for the Normandy invasion, but not one of these articles says anything about what he was doing. Don't you remember hearing about railway transportation, Miranda?"

She nodded. "Vaguely, but I don't have a clue where I heard it. Mother, most likely."

Victoria laughed. "At least I'm not hallucinating."

"I don't think hallucination is an issue," Troy said. "It's not strange that the media wouldn't have access to the details. The senator would have been under orders, so that information would have been classified."

"Get this, Miranda," Victoria said. "It's a picture of Grandfather receiving his medal of honor."

She glanced at the photo of the man who stood impeccably dressed in his uniform while being presented with the medal. Her grandfather had been well into his fifties before Miranda had been born, so she only remembered him as the solemn, white-haired man he was now.

But William Marshall Prescott had been young once, and as she gazed at the image on the screen, she realized that he'd been a stern man even back then. Tall with wavy dark hair even his short haircut didn't hide, he had strong features that were recognizable decades later in the man he'd become.

"Wasn't he handsome?" Victoria sounded dreamy. "I'm rooting for a love story here. I want to hear our grandparents fell in love at first sight. Maybe he even saved her from the concentration camp."

Miranda wasn't surprised that particular fantasy would appeal to her sister.

Dale laughed. "This place has gone to your head."

Victoria waved a dismissive hand. "I'm also hoping for a good explanation for why he refuses to discuss anything about our grandmother. He was probably heartbroken when she died and has never gotten over it."

Even Laura smiled, and when Troy whispered for her ears alone, "We'll keep hoping for that miracle," Miranda smiled, too, feeling much better about this get-to-gether, although she wasn't entirely sure why.

6

THE SUN HADN'T YET risen when Troy heard the knock on the door. Glancing at his watch, he noted the time at precisely oh-five hundred and smiled. Whatever the past grievances between his wife and Laura—and their families for that matter—Laura was an exemplary hostess.

He especially appreciated her effort today. After their dinner last night, he'd caught her in the kitchen and sprang a last minute change in plans on her as a surprise for Miranda. Her arrival proved she'd gone above and beyond the call of duty to make the arrangements, and sure enough, he pulled open the door of his suite to find her dressed in her work uniform, standing beside a push-cart loaded with gear he'd requested.

"Thank you." Troy meant it. "I know this took some work."

She smiled. "That's what I'm here for. I believe I have everything you asked for."

Motioning her in, he stepped aside as she maneuvered the cart through the door. He took stock of the items as she passed. Looked like everything. Backpacks. Thermal cooler.

"Any problem with the clothes?" he asked.

"None at all." Bringing the cart to a stop in the foyer,

she withdrew a neatly folded stack of outdoor wear from the bottom shelf. "Everything should fit her. If not, give me a call, and I'll take care of it so you and Miranda can be on your way."

"How badly have I messed up your plans for the day? If I'd thought about this outing earlier, I'd have arranged it for yesterday. But it didn't occur to me until you mentioned that sunrise fishing tour you had heading out this morning."

"That tour's already on its merry way." Reaching inside her pocket, she lifted out a set of keys. "You and Miranda are my guests, Troy, and as the Hottest Honeymoon Couple, you have privileges, so don't worry about the schedule."

"What about the event you had planned for the Toy Shoppe?"

"I'll reschedule it for another day if you're still interested or we'll simply cancel. It's *your* second honeymoon. Your only job is to have fun." Her smile assured him she meant what she said. "Just make sure you report back to Tyler and your sister-in-law how accommodating we are here at Falling Inn Bed, so we get lots of good press."

"Done. The gear is in the rental?"

"Everything you asked for." She glanced behind him, presumably to see if Miranda was around, then her expression stilled and grew serious. "Thanks again for last night. Given the circumstances, it's not very comfortable when we all get together. I'm sure it wasn't what Miranda expected on her second honeymoon, but I do appreciate the effort on both your parts. If you'll let her know."

Troy appreciated her honesty. "Sorting out this family stuff will turn out to be good all the way around."

"Your mouth to God's ear. Now have a good time today. Do you know where you're going?"

He nodded.

"Then enjoy your picnic. Bruno whipped up something special."

"I'm sure we'll enjoy every bite." And every second of a day spent away from this hotel.

He thanked Laura again, saw her out, then mentally reviewed his plan. Today's mission objective involved getting Miranda away from this hotel and all thoughts of her sister and Laura's investigation. He'd pushed her hard yesterday by agreeing to participate, but she'd adapted quickly and gracefully. Their meeting in Laura's suite last night had been a success.

Today would be a tactical retreat from her family while he forced her to deal one-on-one with him minus the distractions of preplanned events. He'd drawn a parallel between Laura's sunrise fishing expedition and the fishing expedition he was on with his wife and realized they hadn't watched a sunrise together since their trip to Hawaii.

They were going to watch one today. He wanted to remind Miranda of their first honeymoon, the intimacy they'd shared before the stresses of this war had started pulling them apart.

He wanted to veer them from their schedule, too, to keep her reacting spontaneously instead of giving her time to measure her responses. He didn't want to make it easy for her to retreat, wanted to keep her guessing.

Today's trip away from the hotel should do just that.

Making his way into the bedroom, he circled the bed to where she lay fast asleep. The mattress sank as he sat beside her, and his eyes adjusted to the darkness and the sight of her.

Miranda always pulled her hair up while she slept and some had escaped during the night, leaving tendrils curling softly around her face. Her skin had been freshly scrubbed and lotioned before bed, and she looked so lovely, as if her dreams were sweet, and she didn't have a worry.

With her lashes forming dark crescents against her cheeks and her mouth softened in sleep, he saw the woman as she'd always been with him alone—relaxed and natural and at ease.

The way she'd been before letting her defenses creep up between them.

"Wake up, Miranda." He slipped a hand around her jaw, thumbed her cheek, unable to resist the lure of her skin, needing a physical connection to his sleeping beauty.

She exhaled a drowsy sigh that whispered through the darkness, and Troy smiled.

"Time to wake up."

Her peaceful expression melted into a halfhearted frown. She gave a breathy, "Uh-un," then turned and buried her face in the pillow.

He'd expected to meet opposition. "We need to get on the road. I want to watch the sunrise."

It took a while for his words to penetrate but when they did, she said, "Sheet party."

"Change in plans. I sent word that we couldn't make the design your own sexy sheet set party. We'll talk later to decide whether to delay it or cancel."

"Why?"

"So we can go fishing."

That got her attention. One eye cracked open, and she stared without lifting her head off the pillow. "Fishing?"

"Yes."

Her face turned until he found himself staring into her shadowed blue eyes. "As in poles and worms?"

He nodded, gave her an encouraging smile.

Shifting up onto her elbows, she tried to shake off sleep. "I don't understand. You begged off the sheets party?"

"I told Laura we couldn't make it."

"So we can go...*fishing?*"

He nodded, brushing a stray tendril from her temple, unable to resist touching her when her guard was visibly down and she was so clearly trying to make sense of what he'd done.

"What time is it?"

"Just after five."

Her gaze narrowed, but she didn't reply.

"Come on," he said. "If you get up and throw on your clothes, we'll make it in time to see the sunrise over the ridge. I heard it's something we won't want to miss."

"I didn't pack anything to wear fishing."

"All taken care of."

"Laura?"

He nodded, visibly watching her drowsiness melt away as her expression grew more deliberate, composed.

"And when did you make these arrangements?"

"Last night when we were playing one big happy family." He thumbed her lower lip, sorry to see her luscious mouth tighten. "Specifically while you were checking out the lagoon after Victoria mentioned she wanted to get everyone 'straightened out' so she could invite Aunt Suzanne and Uncle Russ to her wedding."

Miranda had slipped away while they'd cleaned up after the meal. Troy knew she needed a few minutes to get away from the group and compose herself. Under normal circumstances, he would have joined her, but last night he'd put his time to better use by asking Laura to arrange this outing.

"Why didn't you mention it?"

"I wanted to surprise you. After everything that happened yesterday, I thought you'd enjoy getting away from the hotel."

"To go fishing?"

"And watch the sunrise like we did in Hawaii."

"Where?"

"North of town. That's all I'll say."

He wasn't about to tell her he'd gone to her sister and Laura for suggestions about where to go. Turned out that Victoria had the perfect place—property of a friend's where they could hike down a ridge and get rustic.

Miranda was obviously less than enthusiastic about this change in plans, but he couldn't tell how much less. She retreated behind that impenetrable mask and seemed reconciled when she asked, "What about a shower? And coffee?"

"Shower later. We'll grab coffee downstairs and drink it on the way."

"I will not leave this room without makeup, Troy. Not negotiable."

Standing, he dragged the covers off her, treated himself to a prime shot of her curves sheathed in a barely there silk nightgown. "Then get a move on. I'll call the restaurant and tell them to start pouring."

Without another word, she slipped out of bed and headed to the bathroom. He watched her go, then made his way to the phone and arranged for coffee pickup. He might be willing to push Miranda out of her comfort zone, but he wasn't crazy enough to wake up his beautiful bride at 5:00 a.m. and not provide caffeine.

THE DAY WASN'T TURNING out to be as hellish as Miranda had expected. They'd caught the sunrise from the ridge, and dawn had broken over the forest in shafts of glorious color that flooded the valley with light. Troy had wrapped his arms around her, and they'd stood in silence, enjoying the sunrise and being together.

She'd managed to rally her enthusiasm and focus on enjoying the day. She wasn't entirely sure what Troy had up his sleeve, but she'd go along if it made him happy. Since he'd graciously consented to play her Tease and Torture game, she could endure fishing or whatever else tickled his fancy. A good marriage was give and take, a balance, and if her husband wanted to fish, she'd make the best of it.

But so far, accommodating Troy's love of the great outdoors wasn't proving to be much of a chore. She could handle getting up at the crack of dawn and hiking down a mountain on a morning as refreshing as this one. The mist hadn't burned away yet and a nip chilled the air as they followed a path down the ridge.

Troy took the lead, brushing aside branches and helping her through rough spots in the trail, and the forest swelled up around them as far as she could see, lush summer foliage shielding them from the rising sun. Wildlife chirped in the trees and rustled—hopefully not *slithered*—in the underbrush, and with Troy marking the trail with his broad shoulders and sure strides, Miranda didn't mind following.

"So how did you hear about this place?" she asked. "It's not a local conservation preserve, is it? I thought all the land around here was privately owned."

"It is."

"Are we allowed to be here?"

"Don't worry. I won't land us in jail."

She just smiled. He might not want to share the details, but it didn't take much of a leap to guess this must have been another collaboration with Laura, *the hostess with the mostest.*

"Like I told you, I wanted to get you away. The hotel's gym and par course is all right, but not especially challenging."

No surprise there. Troy maintained a rigid training schedule, and Falling Inn Bed's facilities couldn't compare to the extreme conditions he was used to. Nor did this wilderness hike remotely resemble her own fitness center back home, which was an upscale spa much in line with the Wedding Wing's new full-service facilities.

Her spa didn't have swarms of gnats that suddenly appeared out of nowhere every time she turned a corner. And her spa was climate controlled with filtered air, so when sweat happened, she wasn't treated to dirt, bits of twigs and corpses of no-see-ums sticking to every inch of exposed skin.

"Have you given any thought to your game plan with the senator?" Troy asked.

Miranda used her sleeve to dab her face. "I'll just ask him about my grandmother and why she changed her name. Keep it simple. If I stick with the cover story and tell him Victoria stumbled across the information while looking into our family history, I might not put him off."

"Sounds like a plan. He might appreciate the warning. A little goodwill wouldn't hurt right now."

"That's for sure. There's probably a very good explanation."

"I'm surprised he hasn't told your mother already."

"For all we know he has. Maybe she just hasn't told us."

"You think so?"

Miranda considered it. Her mother almost never discussed her childhood. Out of deference to her father maybe, or habit. She'd only been six when her mother had died. A lot of years had passed since to sort out her feelings on the subject. "I don't know. It wouldn't surprise me if she didn't know. Grandfather isn't very forthcoming about things he considers private."

"My guess is that's a side effect of his career. Anyone attached to the government has to put on a show. I see it with my dad. He's entirely different in his uniform."

Miranda wouldn't argue the point. Not only had she seen as much with her father-in-law, but with Troy as well. In uniform, her smiling husband who took such pleasure in blindfolding and torturing her with icy sex toys turned into an imposing officer used to giving and taking orders in a rigid chain of command. She knew from his teammates he was well liked, respected and trusted as a good man to have at one's back.

It was the only thing that had been keeping the witchy wives in line. They always managed to be civil when their husbands were around, and Miranda couldn't deny a perverse sense of satisfaction whenever they were forced into different social situations where they had to chitchat politely.

"To be honest, Troy, I don't think I've ever seen my grandfather take off his suit and lighten up. Even when he's with his friends. They're all as imposing as he is. They talk politics and economics, smoke cigars and drink cognac, but they're very private people. I can't recall ever hearing them talk about their families unless it was to announce who got accepted into what college or some other such accomplishment."

Troy crouched down so the fishing rods he wore strapped to his back cleared some low-hanging branches. "Watch your head," he cautioned, making a path so she could pass through. "I'll continue surfing when we get back to the hotel. What time are we due to meet Tyler for our dinner interview tonight?"

"Seven."

Letting the limbs swing back into place, he paused to rearrange the fishing rods that extended a few feet over his head before moving on. "We should be back in plenty of time for me to get online for a while."

Miranda hoped. Casting a glance back over her shoulder, she tried not to think about the return trip. Hiking downhill had to be easier than hiking back up.

"What do you think we'll be able to find out? I was completely flipping out last night with all that talk about classified orders and legal documents. Are you going to be able to find out about Grandfather without anyone getting curious about what you're doing?"

"We only need to know when and where he was stationed during the time we suspect he hooked up with your grandmother. We don't need to know what his orders were. Relax."

Good advice that Miranda knew from experience was easier said than done. But she found herself distracted as their hike wore on, and her backpack seemed to be swelling. The straps dug into her armpits and ribs, and she hitched it up, only to have it drag down again, chafing her skin beneath the cotton shirt that was *supposed* to be absorbing sweat.

She'd be glad once they reached the pond, lake or whatever body of water Troy expected to fish in, so she could end her stint as a pack mule. And eat. Her coffee had worn off long ago, and she'd worked up an appetite that made her stomach growl.

Miranda's spirits improved dramatically when they finally reached the bottom of the ridge and a rapid-running stream with a grassy bank where Troy dropped the gear and made camp.

Slipping out of her backpack, she refused to acknowledge how her husband looked as if he'd barely broken a sweat. She was beyond clammy, not to mention hungry and ready to take a nap before she could even contemplate the next phase of this trek.

Fishing.

She broke out a canteen of water from their gear as Troy hacked off a tree limb, stripping away leaves and plunging into the stream. He picked his way over slimy stones that broke the swift-running current into a series of white-caps, stabbing the stick into the water to test the depth.

"This is going to be great," he said.

She reserved opinion, but couldn't deny that watching him traverse a surefooted path through the water with the sun glinting off his blond hair made the hike down the ridge almost worth the effort. *Almost.*

"I really wish I could appreciate this whole Tarzan of the jungle thing you've got going on, Troy, but I've got to eat before I faint."

"Food's in the backpack," he said. "I'm not sure what, but Laura swore we wouldn't starve."

Miranda glanced inside to find a thermal cooler stuffed with a variety of neatly wrapped finger foods perfect for a picnic. Sandwiches. Salads. Scrumptious-looking iced minicakes. Even plastic cutlery and plates that would be easy to repack for the return journey.

She made do with a few bites of a tastily seasoned pasta salad, returned the containers underneath the ice-packs and went to join her husband, who had unloaded the tackle and now hung a hook on a fishing rod.

"Ready to try your hand at casting?" He smiled when she approached, his crystal gaze raking over her appreciatively when she knelt by his side.

"I feel better knowing we're not going to have to cook and eat what we catch. I was worried. I've never seen this mountain man side of you before."

He laughed. "My father used to take us fishing all the time while we were growing up. Even when we were stationed in Hawaii. Then we'd go out on boats and do the deep sea thing."

"Even Marietta?" Somehow she was having trouble imagining his devil-may-care, jet-setting sister Marietta standing knee-deep in a stream with the sun pounding down on her carefully styled curls.

"Even Marietta. She wouldn't bait a hook or touch

anything she caught. And forget about cleaning a fish. But she loved to get on the bow of the boat and play sun goddess."

"Now that sounds like the Marietta I know and love."

Lying on this grassy bank, tanning in the midday sun sounded like an ideal plan, too, but all things considered, Miranda didn't find fishing so bad.

True, Troy had her standing knee-deep in a stream wearing boots, but the food and the cool water had gone a long way toward refreshing her mood.

Especially when he slipped his arms around her to teach her how to cast her line. She almost forgot about what slimy things might be brushing up against her legs, or the fact that they still had to trudge back up that hill to get back to the rental car.

It was hard to think at all with Troy's body surrounding her, his muscles playing as he guided her arms up and back for the cast, his hips locked against her bottom to secure her against him.

All in all, fishing wasn't so bad when she had her handsome husband to distract her, and she found herself growing aware of the sensual promise in their closeness.

The way he rested his chin comfortably on the top of her head. The sound of his deep even breathing as he instructed her to move slowly to not disturb the water. The way the breeze rippled across the current, carrying with it his familiar scent and proof she hadn't been the only one sweating.

His hands surrounded hers, guided her to toss out the line then draw in the slack. A bright round ball bobbed on the water's surface and then stilled, waiting. Troy showed no signs of letting her go, so she shifted her weight until she balanced against him, enjoying the feel of his arms, his thighs molding her backside.

It was a pleasant moment. They all too seldom had time to enjoy each other anymore, and she remembered back to when they'd been dating. They'd spent lazy days enjoying each other, in bed, out of bed, watching movies, feeding each other—two lovers caught up in the magic of being together.

They somehow never managed time for that anymore. The freedom of those dating years had yielded to the commitments of marriage. Now whenever Troy returned home, he wasn't on leave with nothing better to do than pay attention to her. He had training and officers' functions while she had to get him up to speed with household things that had taken place in his absence.

They usually picked up right where they'd left off, jumping feetfirst into life together without ever taking time to reacquaint themselves the way they'd done while dating.

The *Spouse's Guide to Surviving a Deployment* recommended easing into daily life, taking some time for readjustment away from outsiders and obligations. Maybe she should suggest that they take some time after his next tour of duty. She certainly wouldn't mind spending a few leisurely days in bed with nothing pressing on the calendar.

She filed the thought away. Anything was worth a shot at this point.

"So we just stand here and wait for a fish to swim by and decide he's hungry?" she asked.

"That's the general idea. Relaxing, don't you think?"

More than relaxing, she thought, with the midday sun beating down on them. "Very."

Hiking down a wooded ridge and fishing in a fast-running stream wouldn't have been her first choices for enjoying a summer day with her husband. Then again, she wouldn't have thought she could become aroused while covered in bugs and drying sweat.

But the hard thighs framing her backside and the swelling erection pressing into her lower back were making her very aware of him. And when he leaned down to skim his mouth along her jaw, an openmouthed kiss that made heat pool low in her belly, Miranda found herself titillated more than should have been possible for their current circumstances.

"I can't possibly taste good."

"You *always* taste good." He ran his tongue along the underside of her jaw, a bold stroke that wasn't in the least wary of said bug corpses or sweat. Then he inhaled deeply. "You smell good, too."

Chuckling, she arched her head back to give him better access as he moved his mouth down her throat, pausing to suck lightly on her pulse, which quickened its beat.

"You taste like a woman I want to eat, Mrs. Knight."

Her sex gave a greedy squeeze at the promise in those words, and she forgot all about the icy cold water that had been numbing her feet.

"Are you planning to tease and torture me?"

"I'll surprise you."

"Yay. Another surprise."

He didn't miss her sarcasm and dragged moist hands down her wrists and along her arms, skin brushing skin, sweat combined with grime to lend an unfamiliar friction to the motion that was somehow erotic. "It'll be a good surprise. Hold on to that rod."

She was unaccountably stimulated by the thought of making out in this lush setting, the breeze against her skin and Troy's hands on her. It was a daring thought—someone could happen upon them from the forest's edge along both sides of the stream.

It was also a very unusual thought for her. She didn't have a problem with public displays of affection per se, but she had a big problem with any behavior that had the potential to be misinterpreted or draw criticism.

But this glade seemed like another world entirely. They hadn't seen a soul since long before Troy had steered the rental car off the highway and down a dirt path into the woods. The stream wound under the sunny sky, and while there was nothing to say more fishermen couldn't be standing on the bank somewhere ahead, where the current flowed out of view beneath low hanging branches, Miranda didn't think it likely.

She leaned against him, a deliberate motion that made him brace himself as she ground her bottom against his growing erection. True to form, he didn't need an engraved invitation but met her for the next stroke.

"Feeling frisky, Mrs. Knight?" His deep chuckle found its way to all her sensitive places. "Looking to tease and torture me?"

"That's my surprise." Rising up on tiptoes, she caught his erection in the depression between her cheeks when she rocked her bottom again.

"So two can play this game?"

"Mmm-hmm." And in that moment she wanted nothing more than for him to retaliate.

He did.

Sliding his fingers into the waistband of her shorts, he said, "Wonder what I can reach in here?"

Obviously a rhetorical question. He had already worked his way between her thighs with purpose, zeroing in on the knot of nerve endings that started to ache in anticipation.

"Hold on tight," he said.

Miranda clamped a death grip on the fishing rod as her body went on hyperalert. A sigh slipped from her lips when he reached the target, pressing his thumb against that achy bundle through her cotton panties.

A wave of languid pleasure rolled through her, so intense that she was thoroughly pleased with her game. This was exactly why she'd started up Tease and Torture in the first place—to take away the pressure. They could only do so much standing knee-deep in a stream, and she wouldn't pass up an opportunity to make the most of the moment. If making out in an icy stream was one of Troy's fantasies... She found him surprisingly scrumptious in his sweaty Tarzan mode.

Hanging on to the fishing rod, she ground against him again, smiling when his breath caught, audible proof that the tease part of her game was earning the response she wanted.

He rolled that nub again, a squeeze that made her sex grow warm and moist inside her shorts. Parting her thighs, she gave him better access, but he seemed content to stand there and fondle her with that erotic motion that turned her knees to butter.

Torture, indeed.

Resting her head back against his shoulder, she turned her face until she could reach his neck. Beneath his slightly salty skin was the familiar taste of her husband, the man who could make her respond with only a glance from those cool green eyes.

He was doing more than glancing right now.

Striking up a rhythm that matched that of her rocking bottom, he worked the throbbing place between her thighs until she wanted to laugh at the luxury of the sensation.

No vanishing orgasms here, thank you.

She felt liberated to know they could only touch, arouse and *pleasure*. The rules of her game created set boundaries, dared her to make the most of the moment when fulfillment wasn't in sight.

Such an exhilarating feeling blocked out sight and sound and everything but the feel of his hands, the eager reaction of his body to her steady rocking, his pulse throbbing beneath her mouth. She was barely aware of the fishing pole or the rush of the ice-cold stream around her ankles. Of anything…

Until a crash resounded in the underbrush behind them, shocking the stillness. Instinct made her spin toward the sound, only remembering Troy's hand wedged deep in her shorts when it was too late.

"Miranda!" He hung on to her while trying to pull his arm free and correct them from overbalancing.

She dropped the fishing rod, and by the time she registered the sight of a deer clearing the trees, another behind it, she'd lost her footing on the slippery rocks.

With his well-honed physical reactions, Troy twisted

them away from harm, but with his hand still trapped inside her shorts, the best he could do was break her fall as they went down, plunging into the icy stream.

The water was deep enough to submerge them completely. He absorbed the shock at the bottom then managed to free his hand so they could propel back to the surface. Miranda came up gasping, Troy laughing, both soaking wet and freezing.

"Well, that's one way to cool me down," he said. "What do you call this—the water torture game?"

Miranda thrust dripping hair from her eyes and sucked in a frigid breath. The fishing rod had snagged on a low-hanging branch not far downstream. The deer were long gone.

So much for relaxing. "Well, you knew torture had to be in there somewhere."

7

MIRANDA HANDLED DRYING out on the stream bank better than Troy had expected. Fourteen-thousand-foot sky drops and deep-descent scuba dives were all in a day's work for him. Hiking this ridge with its walkways and shallow stream had been a picturesque stroll. But for Miranda, who worked out in an aerobics class wearing flashy tights, this hike had been a trek into the wilds.

One of the things he loved best about his wife was the femininity that fueled his imagination when he was freezing his ass off during stealth maneuvers. He fantasized about coming home to her. And the reality *always* beat his fantasies.

He found Miranda an easy person to be around, and they shared many common interests. Not to mention that both of them had grown up in family situations that had honed their abilities to perform socially. They were kindred spirits, soul mates.

Despite differing opinions on the great outdoors.

The thought made him smile. He'd known she wouldn't be thrilled with waking up at the crack of dawn to a change in plans. But watching the sunrise had been worth the effort.

True, he hadn't anticipated a dip in the stream, which

had left them sharing their lunch in soggy clothes, but he didn't mind getting wet. She'd rolled admirably with the punches, too, and the only thing better would have been if the water had been warm enough to skinny-dip. *If* he could have convinced Miranda to give it a go. A private beach in Hawaii. A garden tub in the Egyptian Pleasure Pyramid. But a stream in the forest? He would have had to coax her out of her clothes for that. But he could have pulled it off, if he let her know how much it meant to him.

They accommodated each other. That's just the way they did things. He remembered an entire holiday weekend spent trekking through every furniture store in San Diego to redecorate their home, along with hours spent online going over fabric options and even more hours spent on his knees measuring dimensions and arranging floor plans. He would have rather Miranda had taken care of that job while he was away, but she'd wanted his input to make sure he was satisfied with the result.

Fair enough. Their last couch had been too narrow to stretch out comfortably on when he wanted to watch football, and he'd done his share of complaining.

"Let's swing by my mother's," she said. "I want to clean up before we go back to the hotel."

"You're that eager to talk to the senator?" Looked as though he'd accomplished the mission objective better than he'd expected. They hadn't left the ridge yet, and already she was jumping back into the investigation.

"Well that, and I don't want to walk through the hotel with runny mascara and slimy moss in my hair."

Troy didn't see anything that resembled moss, but he couldn't argue the mascara, so after securing the fishing rods tight, he drove them back toward town and asked, "Did getting out today distract you from worrying? Are you feeling better about our investigation?"

Her expression softened. "Today was an…*interesting* distraction. I wouldn't have thought of hiking and fishing myself, but I enjoyed getting away from the hotel and being alone with you."

"But you're worrying again," he said.

She shrugged. "I'm going to keep worrying until this situation plays out. Will you keep my parents occupied while I try to catch Grandfather in his study and warn him about what's going on?"

"Sure. Now will be as good a time as any."

She dabbed away her mascara in the visor mirror. "I don't think there'll be a good time for this conversation, but Naughty Nuptials ends this weekend, so whatever we hope to accomplish has to happen before then. And Victoria's working today. Apparently she and Tyler have cooked up some grand finale, so they have a denouement for their coverage."

"Any idea what?"

"Not a clue. But I'll bet it's outrageous. Those two are peas in a pod. I still can't believe she's engaged to Adam instead of having an affair with Mr. Long-Hair-and-Studs. Adam seems so *normal*."

"Normal is good."

She nodded, sending her damp ponytail bouncing along her shoulders. Without her makeup, she looked fresh and gorgeous, the way she looked in bed. "Just unexpected."

"Maybe she's turning over a new leaf."

"I couldn't say."

"Why else would she choose Adam?"

"She said she's in love, remember? Dinner at my parents?"

Troy wouldn't forget *that* dinner anytime soon, or her family's reaction to the engagement announcement. His own family would have erupted into a clamor he couldn't have heard a siren blast over. Miranda's family had fallen so silent even *he'd* been unnerved.

He had to give Adam a lot of credit for the way he'd addressed that silence, calmly informing everyone that his changing work situation had forced them to consider carefully how best to approach their relationship. He'd explained they were both committed to being together.

Adam had fielded every one of the family's objections without alienating anyone. He hadn't won them over yet, either…except perhaps for Victoria's mother, who apparently recognized how happy her daughter was.

And Troy, too, who only cared how the situation affected Miranda. She seemed content that her future brother-in-law didn't have long hair or any visible studs. That was good enough for him. Add that to the fact that Adam had managed to get across that their engagement wasn't negotiable without having the senator call security, and he'd earned Troy's respect.

"You should talk with your sister, find out why she's suddenly ready to settle down. If it's love at first sight, then maybe Laura is right about miracles around here."

"I suspect they'll need one. Marriage isn't just about love. It requires a lot of work and commitment."

Something about that bothered him. Troy wasn't sure what, her tone perhaps, which struck him as resigned. Or maybe it was the suggestion their marriage didn't come as effortlessly as he thought it did.

"Adam may turn out to be a good influence, Miranda," he said to keep her talking. "He's already gotten your sister to commit. Think about how your parents would feel if she ran off to live with him."

"That's a plus, but I can't say I would have been surprised. What does surprise me is that Victoria hasn't left already. She's talked about moving away for as long as I can remember."

"She must have stayed for a reason. My guess is your family."

"Perhaps, but if that's the case, then why isn't she more involved? Relationships take effort and a good deal of give and take. She could help my father's campaign. As it is, she only shows up when the family has to put on a happy face for the press. Mother spends a lot of time running interference with Grandfather because she's never around."

There it was again... *Relationships take effort and a good deal of give and take.*

Did she really mean *too much* effort?

Shifting his gaze from the road, he found her staring contemplatively out the window, her features etched in delicate lines, her expression closed. She looked lost in thought, and he decided against an interrogation.

"Falling in love might be just what Victoria needs to settle down and save your mom some grief."

"We can hope."

"Yes, we can." And not only for her sister to come around, but for Miranda to open up and talk to him. In an effort to convince her, he slipped his hand over her knee, using touch to bridge the distance. "Love makes people do crazy things."

"We're in love, but we didn't do anything crazy when we got married."

He gave her knee a squeeze. "I'm going to have to disagree with you there, Mrs. Knight."

"What was crazy?"

"You were to marry a man who spends more time away than at home." The truth in that statement cut too close, and Miranda must have known because she slipped her hand over his and squeezed back.

"That's not crazy. What you do is a part of who you are, Troy, and I love everything about you."

"Maybe it's that simple with Victoria and Adam. He needs to accept his job offer and doesn't want to leave her behind."

"Touché." She inclined her head, a gesture that let him admire the way her damp hair glistened in the sunlight streaming through the windshield. "I'll try to keep an open mind."

And so would he because she'd just given him a big piece of the puzzle with her talk about marriage and commitment and work.

He just needed to figure out where it fit.

WHILE MIRANDA FRESHENED up to meet with her grandfather, she considered her best approach and decided straightforward was her safest choice. She fully expected his explanation to be a simple one. If she was entirely honest, she needed it to be. She wanted his guidance on how to proceed, so they could put this whole business behind them without any major explosions or long-term consequences.

If her mother chose to resume relations with Laura's

mother, she'd know best how to handle the situation. Miranda didn't have a problem with that, so she couldn't figure out why she felt so stressed.

Yes, they were dragging up past history and potentially painful secrets, but it felt like so much more. Was she just raw because of everything happening in her life? Or was performing damage control forcing her to deal with uncomfortable emotions.

Like guilt. Victoria didn't need any more trouble right now. She'd already reached her quota for the week with her impromptu engagement.

Yet Miranda couldn't ignore her responsibility, either. She saw too many potential pitfalls where Victoria had chosen not to look. If she'd just been able to go to her mother…but Victoria and Laura were right on this point. They shouldn't raise questions they couldn't answer. Not about this sensitive subject.

No, Miranda had landed smack in the middle of this situation without many choices. But she knew what she had to do, and while hurrying down the back stairway toward her grandfather's study, she told herself she could handle this. She could pretty up her explanation so she wasn't throwing Victoria to the wolves.

She knocked on the door, then after a brief pause heard him call out an invitation. Slipping inside, she tried to shake off her nerves.

William Marshall Prescott's study was a rich-looking room with black walnut furniture, paneled walls, a massive fireplace and lots of books behind glass doors. Miranda had always thought the Gothic mood reflected the man himself.

She wouldn't deny that he had a hard reputation,

even within their family. Age and maturity had allowed her to appreciate that, while her grandfather might be stern, he was also an admirable man, one who stuck to his principles and fought for his beliefs, no matter what the opposition.

He wasn't sitting behind his desk as was his norm, but standing at the window staring out at the back lawn, where Miranda knew summer had overtaken the grassy slope leading down to the lake. Ducks would be swimming in lazy circles or napping on the bank, and the few flowering bushes her grandfather permitted on the grounds would be bright splashes of color in an otherwise manicured green world.

"Grandfather, do you have a minute?" She resisted the impulse to whisper that she always had inside this room.

A member of the Senate for more decades than she'd been alive, her grandfather had the gift of projecting his presence, and as he turned toward her, catching her with a gaze so dark it was almost black, his hands still held clasped on his cane, Miranda was struck by how the years hadn't diminished him at all. She could still see that young hero Victoria had shown her beneath the shock of white hair and the stoic expression.

"What can I do for you, Miranda?"

"I wanted to talk with you."

"About your sister?"

"Yes, as a matter of fact. How did you know?"

He only motioned to a chair in front of his desk. "Please have a seat." Circling his desk, he propped his cane against the wall, sat before her and said, "Go on."

Being the focus of that still black gaze brought back memories of various lectures she'd received sitting in front of this desk. Lectures about infractions, or life lessons, or worldly happenings. Her grandfather had never been a physically demonstrative man, but once she'd moved past early childhood, he'd shared the values and ideals that had been instilled upon generation after generation of the Prescott family. Her last name might be Ford, but her blood ran true Prescott as far as her grandfather was concerned.

She took a deep breath and said, "I want to ask you a question."

He inclined his head and waited.

"We've been researching our family genealogy on-line." She borrowed Victoria's cover story and side-stepped her sister's name in favor of a royal *we.* "Since we've been together so much during this visit, we decided to see what we could find. With the Internet, information is so accessible."

"If you were interested in the family, why didn't you ask me? I've always been forthcoming."

No doubt there. Her grandfather had always willingly shared his side of the family. Miranda even had memories of her now-deceased great-grandmother telling stories about how the Prescotts arrived from England to involve themselves in this country's politics while there'd only been thirteen colonies.

"I know that." Miranda steeled herself to give the answer she knew he wasn't going to like. "But we had some questions about Grandmother that we didn't want to trouble you with."

Although his expression never changed, his reaction flared in his gaze—shock, disapproval and *something else* she couldn't identify but sensed boded ill.

"You've been researching information about your grandmother on the *Internet*," he repeated and there was no missing his disapproval about the public forum they'd chosen for their search.

Unfortunately this wasn't anything Miranda hadn't already thought of herself, so she just nodded, giving him a chance to absorb her news.

If possible, his expression grew even more remote, and she was struck by how isolated he suddenly seemed, as if his dignity and self-possession kept him removed from any type of emotional reaction to bombshells like this one....

Or from anyone who might dare to come close.

"What questions?"

"We were curious about Grandmother's name. We came across some documentation that suggested she came from France and had Americanized her name."

There, she'd phrased that about as diplomatically as she could because she wasn't about to confront him with two marriage certificates, both with his signature on them.

When he didn't answer, Miranda wasn't sure he'd understood her question. "I wasn't sure why our grandmother would Americanize her name, but I knew there must have been a reason. I'm bringing this to your attention to make sure we aren't opening up a can of worms that is best left closed."

Her words faded to a silence so complete that she could hear the antique clock on the mantel—a clock that had made the journey over from England with one of her ancestors, in fact—tick with a steady rhythm that mirrored her own heartbeat pounding too loudly in her ears.

Miranda didn't breathe and couldn't be sure her grandfather did, either, but as she stared into his unreadable face, she made a mental note to hunt down and kill her sister and Laura as soon as she got back to the hotel.

Troy, too. She did not like running interference for a cause she didn't believe in, and that had nothing to do with principles. It had everything to do with the accusation she felt radiating off her grandfather right now, for feeling responsible for creating conflict with the people she loved.

Rising from behind his desk, he pushed himself to his feet, a move that appeared to require monumental effort. He braced his hands on the edge to steady himself, his black gaze boring into hers.

"I'm surprised at you, Miranda." He paused, giving her a chance to absorb the weight of his words and his tone, one she remembered so well, a tone that had always made her feel as if she hadn't disappointed only him, but countless generations of faceless ancestors. "You don't usually let your imagination run away with you. That behavior is classic Victoria."

Miranda knew no reply was necessary, so she just waited, willing herself to breathe again.

"You and your sister have made a mistake." He continued. "You've obviously traced information about the wrong woman. Your grandmother's name was Laura Russell. There is no question and no *can of worms*." His tone grew steadily more clipped, more unyielding. "Anything you want to know about her, I will tell you. No more searches on the Internet. Do you understand?"

She understood he'd just passed an edict about public genealogy searches. She understood that to continue the search would be to defy his expressed wishes.

But she didn't understand how she was supposed to trust him when he'd just lied to her.

Miranda had seen copies of the marriage documents—one from an obscure little church in the French countryside, the other from a well-known church in London. She'd seen his signature beside his bride's.

Laure Roussell.

And she understood that whatever he didn't want them to know about their grandmother was serious enough to make a man renowned for his blunt honesty lie to her without flinching.

And he didn't flinch. He faced her with the same strength of purpose she'd recognized in Victoria's photograph last night. But he wasn't the same man. Suddenly Miranda noticed every line on his face, the way his wavy white hair had started to thin at the temples, and the question she wanted an answer to faded on her lips.

And that was when she understood just how much she didn't like confrontation, didn't like facing the ugly, uncertain way she felt right now.

She could have asked him about his signature on the marriage licenses. She'd seen them, for goodness' sake, proof that the marriage had taken place twice. But she couldn't come up with any way to ask that didn't sound like an accusation.

So she didn't say anything at all, hid the knowledge she had, telling herself that he must have a good reason, even though she didn't quite believe it.

"I'd caution you against following in your sister's footsteps right now." His dark gaze sliced the distance between them, his tone cut.

She could see no trace of the calm-voiced grandfather who had taught her about politics and economics while she'd grown up, the demanding, challenging man who shared his opinions and enjoyed discussing hers. In his place was an old man whose expression had closed up like a fist.

"Victoria's making choices that are running her into trouble, and you don't want to go along for the ride. Her engagement was impulsive enough, but making a spectacle of herself at a wedding—"

"Wedding?" The only thing that had been saving Victoria was that the family hoped her engagement would be a reasonable one. "She's set the date?"

He inclined his head, an oh-so regal gesture that sent a chill along her spine. "Your sister has informed us that her wedding will be the grand finale of the inaugural campaign she's covering."

It took a few seconds for his words to register, for Miranda to comprehend that making the wedding the grand finale would mean getting married *this* weekend.

Then she could only stare at her grandfather, not having a clue what to say, but knowing with a wild certainty that she'd just made a bad situation worse.

Much, much worse.

8

TROY HAD LEARNED about Victoria's plans for a weekend wedding while Miranda had still been talking to the senator. By the time he'd seen her, she'd been so withdrawn that she'd explained what had happened during her visit to the senator's study in less than twenty seconds.

He understood she felt telling the senator about their investigation had made the situation worse and offered to reschedule their dinner interview with Tyler for another night. But in true Miranda fashion, she'd reined her emotions in tight and insisted she'd be fine.

She was more than fine. She'd slipped behind her perfect persona and wowed Tyler all through dinner. She'd been charming, informative and her performance so *on* that he'd never have known she'd just walked away from a family mess.

She was still *on* when they said their goodbyes after dinner, and Troy escorted her back to their suite, barely able to make out his wife behind the too-composed features.

"How are you holding up?" he asked.

She glanced at him, her face shadowed as they passed beyond the wall sconces that illuminated the hall. "Fine. And you?"

She might have appeared fine, but she wasn't. She'd only put aside her feelings about the day's events, and he wasn't happy that she was trying to sell him otherwise. Did she expect him to buy her reassurances?

He wasn't letting her off the hook so easily. "What are we doing about your sister? Helping your mother pull together a wedding in a few days?"

"If I'm understanding this right, Mother won't have to do a thing. Victoria's wedding will be a Falling Inn Bed promotional stunt, which means Laura and her staff will host. Although I can't guess whom Victoria thinks will come on such short notice, I guess that's not my problem."

"Your mother seemed to think that making the wedding part of the Naughty Nuptials will minimize the need for explanations. She said Victoria will be making the announcement in her article tomorrow morning." He inserted the keycard in the door, and added, "Your mom seemed fine with the news."

In fact, his mother-in-law had seemed as fine as Miranda did now.

"She has no choice but to make the best of the situation," Miranda said.

"She also said she didn't think the senator would have much of a choice but to accept Victoria's plans, either."

But the senator did have another choice—the very same choice he'd made with his own daughter thirty years earlier.

None of them had said it aloud, but there wasn't a question in Troy's mind they'd all been thinking it. And debating what to do if the senator severed ties with his youngest granddaughter.

But what he remembered most was the way his mother-in-law had put on the appearance of everything being all right. There'd been no media around, no one but family, yet she'd put on an award-winning performance.

Miranda was doing the same thing, and had been all day. She'd smiled when he'd taken her hiking and fishing then again at dinner with Tyler. Troy couldn't help but think…how was he ever supposed to know how she really felt?

They entered the suite, and if he hadn't been watching so closely, he would have missed the signs of her relief, the sigh, the way she rubbed her temples to soothe away an ache.

He was still watching when she disappeared into the bedroom, only to reappear a few moments later sans shoes and jacket. Her face was so composed, her deep blue gaze shuddered in a way he knew hid how she felt.

"Will you do the honors?" Turning her back, she piled shiny curls on top of her head so he could reach her zipper.

Unfastening her dress, a sheath in a deep ruby-red that complemented her dark hair and fair skin, he parted the fabric to reveal her lacy chemise and the slim curve of her waist. She glanced back over her shoulder and smiled.

"Thanks."

She sounded totally normal, and he wanted to know how often he'd let her smile divert him from how troubled she really was. Catching her before she got away, he pulled her to him and lifted her into his arms.

"Troy!" She abandoned the attempt to hold on to her dress, and threaded her arms around his neck. "What are you doing?"

"I'm putting you in bed. You've had a long day."

"I need to check in with my mother—"

"In the morning."

"But we need to discuss how to handle Grandfather—"

"Tomorrow." A command that wasn't negotiable.

And Miranda obviously recognized it because she only rolled her eyes as he marched her into the bedroom and deposited her on the bed.

"I'm not ready to go to sleep yet," she pointed out.

"No problem."

He was on her in a second, pulling her hard against him, until all her barely-covered-in-silk curves unfolded against him. Her hair tumbled around them, draping them in silky curls. His pulse shot straight into the red zone, and he wished he was naked to feel every inch of her enticing body.

To tease and torture an honest reaction out of her.

"I thought you were putting me to bed." Her breathy voice belied her cool expression.

"No reason I can't join you." Burrowing his knee beneath hers, he flipped her onto her stomach in a neat move she obviously didn't see coming.

With a gasp, she propped up on her elbows, but he straddled her, pinning her beneath him. "What are you doing now?"

"I'm making you feel better."

"I feel fine."

"Yes, you do."

She gave a huff as he drew up her slip, peeling away the fabric to reveal the smooth skin below. Unhooking her bra, he directed her arms above her head to remove everything until she lay beneath him with only her shimmery hose covering her heart-shaped bottom and her legs.

"You are too tempting, Mrs. Knight."

Running his fingers along her spine, he smiled when she shivered, an immediate reaction that reassured him. Whatever might be going on inside her head, she still felt as deeply for him as ever. They were magic together.

"Oh, that feels nice." She exhaled the words. "So what did I do to deserve this special treatment?"

"You let me take you fishing."

"It wasn't so bad."

He wished he could believe her, but he thought she was just making the best of the situation to please him. Like she'd done with Tyler at dinner. Like she was doing right now.

Sweeping her hair over her shoulder, he massaged her neck with a firm motion. "Just relax and let me do my thing."

"Mmm," was her only reply as he worked his thumbs into her muscles, kneading away the tension there.

He loved touching her. Even now, when all wasn't well, they were still comfortable together in a way he'd never been with anyone else.

He wanted her to feel that way, too. Comfortable enough to share how she felt.

For better or worse.

He'd meant the vows he'd made inside this hotel nearly two years ago. But if she only shared the *better* and hid the *worse*… He needed to prove he'd stick by her side and love her no matter what.

It didn't take long to put her to sleep. He worked over

her tense muscles with steady strokes until her lashes fluttered shut and her mouth parted around even breaths. He'd dragged her down a ridge at sunrise, into a stream and back again, and if the physical activity hadn't been enough to wear her out, her performances throughout the day had finished the job.

Covering her with the satin comforter, he slipped out of the bedroom and headed straight for the computer. He had another piece of the puzzle and a few big questions to answer.

When did Miranda get to be herself? And with whom?

While he was away, he only knew what she shared on their Web site and in her phone calls and letters.

Logging on to Knights Online, he began surfing through the archives of more than a year's worth of bulletin board entries. He searched for clues about what had been going on in Miranda's social life at home.

The answers had to be in here.

Scrolling through entry after entry, he read reports of the day-to-day business she took care of in his absence. She'd hired a new lawn maintenance service, dealt with a necessary financial transfer with their advisor, dismantled their living room to texture the walls with a technique she'd learned in a class at the local hardware superstore.

He recalled the news she'd been relaying about her father's career, a recent visit from her mother, her best friend Joan's pregnancy. She wrote about his family as enthusiastically as she did about her own, but she never mentioned any friends except those she'd left behind on the East Coast.

Troy frowned down at the screen. Now that he

thought about it, he hadn't noticed her socializing with any of his buddy's wives, either. They all got together for functions while he was home, but no matter how hard he combed his memory, he couldn't recall her ever exchanging anything more than pleasantries with any of the women in their social circle.

A red flag started waving, and he kept skimming the posts, looking for any mention of get-togethers with friends off base. He found the occasional mention of wives' club meetings, students she corresponded with through her online Web design classes and her trainer at the fitness center.

No mention of shopping with girlfriends or weekday luncheons or anything to suggest she'd been making friends in their new home.

Sitting back in the chair, Troy rubbed his neck to ease the tension. Why didn't she mention who she spent time with while he was away?

Was there anyone to mention?

He frowned. They'd been stationed in San Diego for almost a year now, plenty of time to settle into their life.

He thought back on his own childhood, the moves from base to base, so many through the years that most blurred together. The orders arrived on the military's timetable, and sometimes that timing worked, sometimes it didn't.

He remembered the year his dad's tour took him overseas. The family got to accompany him that time, but Troy had been barely two months away from graduating middle school and had been training hard with his hockey team.

The solution had been for his grandmother to live

with him in their big house, newly furnished with rental furniture, until he wrapped up the year and graduated. She'd dragged him to every practice and sat through each game until his team had won the play-offs.

Sure those moves had turned out to be an adventure that he'd eventually learned to appreciate. He had five siblings who were a constant through every relocation and by necessity he'd learned to settle in and make new friends fast. He'd had a lifetime to hone his skills, and when he thought of Miranda's upbringing...

Troy had always believed that her family situation had prepared her for the unique demands of marriage to an officer, but she'd also grown up in one house and one town. They hadn't celebrated their second anniversary yet and had already moved twice, this latest time clear across the country. Had she honestly had enough time to develop the knack of settling in fast?

The pieces seemed to fall into a place that made too much sense, which left him wondering how he could have been so blind.

If Miranda hadn't settled in yet, she was likely feeling isolated and alone during his absences, which would certainly explain her withdrawal. It would also explain the perfect world she'd created online, a fantasy place where he could log on and be reassured that his wife and their life were right where he'd left them.

But it didn't explain why she wouldn't just tell him there was a problem.

So how could he find out who she was interacting with at home without letting her know he was looking?

He needed reinforcements...well, one reinforcement who could help him get some information without being obvious, one who understood what life as his wife would entail better than anyone.

Glancing at the computer clock, Troy calculated what time it would be in Nebraska, then reached for the phone.

"Hello, Mom…"

9

"So what happened to you last night?" Miranda asked with a yawn when she left the bedroom to find Troy seated at the desk with a mug of steaming coffee by his side.

Mmm, caffeine.

She didn't wait around for an answer but followed her nose into the kitchen where half a pot remained. Pouring a cup, she made her way back into the living room.

Troy had spun the chair around and sat watching her, looking perfectly wide-awake and freshly showered. "I wondered if you were ever going to get up this morning."

"You put me into a coma with that massage. I had no idea you could do that."

"I usually try to arouse you, not put you to sleep."

If the muscles in her face had been awake, she might have laughed, but talking proved enough of an effort. "So I passed out, and you left."

"You relaxed, I got aroused. Since I couldn't sleep, I got up to see what I could find on the senator. I figured I wasn't going against his wishes since I researched him and not your grandmother."

"A technicality at best." Sinking down onto the sofa, Miranda stretched out and sipped her coffee, sighing as the hot brew seared a path down her throat. This caffeine needed to kick in fast if she was going to wake up thinking about yesterday. "So, did you come up with anything?"

He raked his gaze over her, a slight smile touching his lips, and she knew he was enjoying the sight of her rumpled and half-asleep. "Sure did. Turns out the senator was a BEL."

"What's a bell?"

"B-E-L, as in behind enemy lines. The Americans and British pooled resources to create a unit of special forces teams to send into occupied France and assist the French Resistance."

"I learned about all this in school, but I've never heard word one in regard to my grandfather."

"Classified."

"Can you get in trouble over this, Troy?"

He shot her a look of bravado that didn't reassure her one bit. "This information was classified during World War II, now it's part of our military history. If one knows where to look."

"I honestly don't know that you should look. My grandfather expressly told me to stop digging around."

"*You* weren't digging around. Do you want me to tell you what the BELs did or do you want to discuss how to handle this situation now the cat's out of the bag and we've got a problem?"

"Boy, do we ever have a problem." The lure of the sofa called, and she let her head sink back into the cushions and closed her eyes, her whole body sluggishly resisting the warm rush of caffeine. Here she thought her biggest problem would be keeping up the Tease and Torture game so she didn't ruin the last week of their trip.

Life was just full of surprises lately.

"Why don't we forget that we ever got involved with any of this insanity and head home early?" she suggested, not missing the irony of running back to the witchy wives when she'd tried to escape them on this vacation.

"What about damage control?"

"Oh, we're off to a great start." She didn't bother opening her eyes and waved a dismissive hand. "I've made things a thousand times worse already."

"You couldn't have known what Victoria had planned, so I don't think it's time to run and hide just yet."

Run and hide? She cracked an eyelid and tried to glare. "I don't want to aggravate the situation, Troy. That's different than running and hiding."

The man didn't look even remotely remorseful. "What do you think the senator will do about the wedding? He doesn't have the sort of power he had over Laura's mother. I don't think Victoria will care much one way or the other if he takes away her trust fund, do you?"

"She'd probably think life without her trust would be an adventure. Not that Adam looks like he's hurting for money."

"If the senator decides to break off with your sister, all he can really do is ask her to move out of the house and force you all into a situation where you'll have to choose what to do about her wedding." He held her gaze steadily. "Are you prepared to make that choice?"

She nodded, supposing on some level she'd known this was coming. She just hadn't been ready to deal with the truth yet, had hoped there'd be a way to save the day.

Unfortunately she'd nixed that possibility when she'd walked into her grandfather's study.

She *shouldn't* feel as if her loyalties were divided. Victoria started all this craziness, joining forces with Laura, and getting married to a man she'd met a few weeks ago.

"So what will you do?" Troy asked.

Forcing her eyes open, she sat up and took another fortifying sip of coffee. "I'll do whatever's best for the family."

"Any idea what that is?"

"Not a clue. I only know what's not best. Forcing my mother to choose between her daughter and her father."

"I don't think it'll do anything for Victoria, either." He folded his arms across his chest and asked bluntly, "If the senator makes a stand, will you let your sister go?"

Her brain cells weren't firing yet, because it took a moment to understand what Troy was asking, and when she did, the implication in his question rubbed her the wrong way.

She didn't want to make this choice, didn't want any more ugly confrontations, and didn't like how this made her feel—as if she wanted to...

Run and hide.

Troy's words echoed in her head. Is that what he thought she was doing? Was she?

"How can I let Victoria go when I don't have her?" She felt as uncertain as she had yesterday in her grandfather's study, as unable to deal with the situation. She hated the way that felt. "I've never had her. We're not close like you and Marietta."

"Are you angry with her?"

"I'm not exactly thrilled she's got the whole family in an uproar *again*," she said. "Why can't she just make the effort to get along? Especially now. We'll be going home next week, and if she goes through with this wedding, she'll be leaving town sooner than any of us expected. The last thing my mother needs is trouble with Grandfather."

"I think that's her point, Miranda. She wants to bring the family back together so your mother won't be alone. That's what Laura wants for her mother, too."

"Then why can't she go about it like a *normal* person?"

Troy laughed. "Hate to break it to you, sweetheart, but there's not a normal person in your family."

Miranda wouldn't dignify *that* with a response and massaged her temples. A dull ache had started, and she hadn't even brushed her teeth yet. Great.

Dragging down another long gulp of coffee, she tried to decide if more coffee would do the trick or if she needed to get a jump on this headache with some gel-tabs. She hadn't decided yet when a knock sounded on the door.

Forgetting all about caffeine or geltabs, Miranda flung herself off the sofa and raced into the bedroom. "I don't care who it is. I'm in the shower."

But she hadn't made it into the bathroom before she heard her sister say, "Good, then she'll be a captive audience."

Miranda barely had a chance to register the steel in Victoria's voice before she appeared in the bedroom doorway. Slamming the door shut behind her, she cut off Troy, who clearly wasn't invited. Then she bore down on Miranda, all dark scowl and wild red hair.

"You narced on me."

A few of Miranda's brain cells started working—enough to convince her there was no escape.

"How could you tell grandfather what I was doing?" Victoria demanded, and Miranda took a deep breath, resolved not to get sucked into an angry confrontation.

She *had* narced on Victoria. And it wasn't her sister's fault that she hadn't had enough caffeine yet to offset the headache looming in her immediate future, either.

Or that she hadn't even brushed her teeth.

No, Victoria wasn't responsible for any of that, and one of them had to keep calm. But it wasn't easy when her sister was one of those people who existed on adrenaline. Victoria could stay up late, wake up early or not sleep at all and appear to suffer no effects. Which meant she looked as fresh as if she'd been up and about for hours, while Miranda felt as though she could barely crawl on her hands and knees to get away.

"I didn't tell Grandfather what *you* were doing," she said, pleased with how reasonable she sounded. "I told him *we* were researching our family history and had come across some questions about our grandmother."

"But why would you do that? Now he knows we're digging around. He called me and laid on this whole guilt trip about how I was dividing ranks in the family and I needed to stop—"

"I had an obligation. I understand what you're trying to do and I agreed to participate. But, Victoria, regardless of how well intentioned you are, there are still potential consequences. Our grandmother changed her name, so there was a reason. Grandfather is the only person who knows what that reason is and whether or not it should stay hidden. You don't want some ancient bomb to blow up in Mother's face. I know you don't."

"I heard all your objections the other night, Miranda. I was sitting in the room, remember? And you heard me promise to be careful. I said I wouldn't do anything to invite questions."

"But you can't guarantee that."

Victoria leaned back against the dresser and folded her arms across her chest, a defensive gesture if ever Miranda saw one. But it wasn't until she gazed into her sister's face that she realized defense wasn't the issue at all.

"No, you're right." The anger drained from Victoria's voice. "I can't guarantee that. Just like I can't guarantee I'll be alive in the morning. But I told you I would do everything in my power to cover my tracks. You didn't trust me."

"It's not about trust—"

"No?" The word ached the way she said it. "What is it, then? You obviously don't credit me with enough intelligence to do some research—which is my job, incidentally—without screwing up."

No, defense wasn't the issue at all here—hurt was. And Miranda felt the weight of her power to hurt in that moment more than she'd ever felt it before.

You're the big sister, Miranda. It's your job to keep an eye on Victoria, to protect her if she needs protecting, her mother's words replayed in her memory from a long-ago childhood. *That's what big sisters do.*

She could hear that soft-spoken voice in her head, but all she could see was the hurt in Victoria's face.

"I'm sorry." The apology fell flat between them,

sounding inadequate and lame. "I wasn't trying to get you into trouble."

"Don't." Victoria gestured a hand dismissively, and her expression faded, replaced by a steel that Miranda was much more familiar with.

Much more *comfortable* with.

"I knew this would be a stretch when I asked you to help," Victoria said soberly. "I knew you didn't like Laura, and I knew you didn't have any faith in what's happening around Falling Inn Bed. I asked you anyway. That was my choice. I thought I could convince you to give me a chance. I was sure I could get you past your everything-has-to-go-perfectly-according-to-plan attitude. I was wrong."

For a moment, Miranda could only stare. "What are you talking about? Just because you and I have different ways of going about things doesn't mean—"

"Miranda, please," she said. "You don't have to defend yourself. Especially to me. I gambled. I lost. No big deal."

But if it wasn't a big deal then why did the look on her face make Miranda's stomach knot up tight?

"The only thing we have to decide is what to do now that Grandfather has issued his ultimatum," Victoria said.

"What ultimatum?"

"If I continue 'dividing the ranks' as he puts it, he'll boycott my wedding and expect you all to do the same."

Miranda sank onto the edge of the bed. "He said that?"

Victoria nodded.

She closed her eyes to block out the sight of that wounded expression on her sister's face, but only exchanged it for the image of Victoria dressed in an exquisite white gown, standing beside Adam Grant in a ballroom filled with empty chairs. Maybe it was an aftereffect of spending the past few weeks immersed in all the wedding events of the Naughty Nuptials, but Miranda could see the picture as if it was 3-D.

But even that image wasn't as bad as the tone of resignation in her sister's voice. They might not be especially close, but Miranda knew Victoria didn't expect anyone in their family to support her.

And she'd resolved to accept and make the best of it.

An ability that connected them, marked them as members of a family that put on a smile no matter what.

"Are you really so surprised?" Victoria's voice caught softly, as if she felt bad because Miranda seemed so shocked. "You shouldn't be. This has been coming for a long time."

"Then why don't you stop this craziness now? Or do you want no one to show up at your wedding?"

"But someone will be coming, Miranda. That was going to be part of my surprise."

A *Victoria* surprise was enough to make her blood run cold. "We haven't had enough surprises for now?"

"A matter of opinion. I happen to like surprises." She shrugged. "So what will you do if Grandfather boycotts me?"

"What surprise?"

"Laura and Dale are getting married with Adam and me. We're having a double wedding."

Maybe dealing with the witchy wives and vanishing orgasms had worn her down. Maybe she was becoming unhinged from nearly three weeks at Falling Inn Bed, a hotel that had proven itself more asylum than romance resort, but at this moment Miranda wanted nothing more than to walk out that bedroom door, collect her husband and hop on a plane.

And where was her husband? He'd obviously abandoned her because there was nowhere he could hide in this suite to avoid overhearing this exchange. He knew there was trouble, yet he'd chosen to stay away.

"I can't believe you're all caught up in this insanity so much that you'd get *married* to hook readers. Marriage is a serious commitment, Victoria. I know. I'm married."

"I understand that, which is why I've been single."

"But you're marrying a man you've only known a few weeks."

Victoria exhaled heavily. "You're entitled to interpret that however you want. I won't waste your time trying to change your mind. But I will say that just because it has taken me less time to decide what I want with Adam doesn't invalidate my feelings, or make me reckless. I understand my history is working against me here, and I respect that. But things with Adam are different."

"If you really feel that way, then why don't you slow down, have a reasonable engagement and set a date. Problem solved."

"Except that Adam's leaving Niagara Falls to take a new job in Las Vegas."

"Troy and I established our relationship long distance. We live long distance a great deal of the time now."

Victoria pushed away from the dresser, and turned away. "Life's too short to waste time trying to make everyone else happy. I want to be happy. You're the selfless one. And I'm not perfect like you, remember?"

Those words were so rich with emotion that Miranda

found herself too shocked to speak. She sat there blinking stupidly with her head about to explode.

"*Perfect.* Oh, *please.*" She shoved the words out. "What on earth is that supposed to mean?"

"Why don't we just leave things for now, Miranda? I don't want to make the situation worse. It's not part of the plan."

"What plan? The plan where you give Grandfather a heart attack so he drops dead on the floor?"

"The plan to get our families back together." Victoria still didn't turn around. "A big wedding will be a happy occasion to get our mothers together."

"Let's come up with another plan because this one is alienating the half of the family that still talks." Forcing herself off the bed, Miranda went to stand beside her sister, to establish some sort of closeness, if only proximity. "I asked Grandfather point-blank why Grandmother changed her name, and do you know what he told me?"

Victoria finally looked at her, and Miranda recognized the glint of tears in her eyes. She wanted to say something, *do* something to wipe away that look. A look that told her Victoria was getting exactly the reaction she'd expected and was determined to deal with it.

But Miranda didn't know what to do, so she said, "He told me we were researching the wrong woman."

"And you believed him?"

She shook her head. At least she could give her sister that. "No. You showed me the marriage licenses, and I don't question his signature. But I do question why this is important. You should have seen him, Victoria. He was so old. I don't know why he's lying, but I know he has a reason. He'd never lie otherwise. Not Grandfather."

"Let's cut to the chase. Do you want me to drop everything and give up any hope of getting all of us back together?"

Victoria made *everything* sound wildly out of balance with the happiness of one man. But it wasn't just one man, Miranda reminded herself. It was safeguarding her mother from potential heartache, her father from public grief if their investigation breathed life into an old scandal on the eve of a campaign.

"Why are you asking me to decide? I'm not going to tell you whether or not you should get married."

"Good, because I'm getting married. Whether I do it as part of the Naughty Nuptials or not is my choice. Just like whether you choose to attend is yours. Do you want me to call off the search?"

"Honestly, given all this trouble, I don't see how knowing the truth can help."

"You do realize that I didn't expect to find a skeleton when I started looking, don't you? Laura and I were trying to understand what happened, so we could figure out the best way to fix the problem without giving Grandfather a heart attack."

"And I didn't expect Grandfather to make a stand when I told him what we were doing. I expected a simple explanation. If there was anything to worry about, I figured he'd tell me how to perform damage control."

"Damage control," Victoria repeated, the words so void of emotion that Miranda knew instantly they'd been a mistake.

"What if our grandmother ran off with another man and was killed?" she said quickly, needing to explain, to wipe away that blank look from her sister's face, a defense that revealed so much more than anger ever could. "Maybe Grandfather has been lying all these years to *protect* our mothers. Learning about an awful truth won't do anything but hurt them."

She didn't question that her reasoning was rational. But *rational* didn't take away the look on Victoria's face, a look that swelled into one of those rare sister moments when implications reached far beyond the words, and feelings were hurt in ways that only happened between sisters—close or not.

A moment when Victoria understood that Miranda hadn't believed her capable of conducting a search without an unpleasant fallout, that she'd judged her plan as nothing more than a way to stir up trouble, and hadn't trusted her judgment at all.

A moment when Miranda felt like the worst sister on the planet.

You're the big sister, Miranda. It's your job to keep an eye on Victoria, to protect her if she needs protecting, her mother had said. More words. *That's what big sisters do.*

Not this big sister.

This *perfect* sister had just convinced Victoria she was an irresponsible, devil-may-care rebel, who'd crossed enemy lines to collude with Laura to fix a decades-old problem she didn't even understand.

"I won't be responsible for 'dividing the ranks' or giving Grandfather a heart attack." Victoria accepted the verdict with style and grace. "As of this second, the search is off. I'll take care of Laura. I'll sign a contract in blood or whatever will satisfy Grandfather. Are you happy now?"

Miranda should be. *Her* problem was solved. If Victoria stopped the search, their grandfather wouldn't make a stand and she wouldn't have to choose whether or not to attend the wedding.

She wouldn't have to deal with any more ugly emotions.

But Miranda wasn't happy. Perhaps it was Victoria's expression, or the resignation in her tone…but this acquiescence didn't feel anything like a victory.

Before Miranda could figure out how to react, Victoria demonstrated more grace-under-fire by assuming control.

"I'll let sleeping dogs lie," she said. "But I won't sacrifice my happiness to satisfy this family's expectations of acceptable behavior. Adam and I are getting married on Saturday along with Laura and Dale. We're celebrating together and wrapping up the Naughty Nuptials. We're going to give our mothers the opportunity to be together in a positive situation if they want to. I'd like my family with me and happy for me."

She paused, drawing a deep breath and steeling herself before Miranda's very eyes.

"Victoria, I—" She wanted nothing more in that moment than to say the right thing, to say *anything* to let Victoria know she did wish her happiness. "I don't think—"

"Hear me out, Miranda," she said. "I've put all of you in a tough position. I didn't always understand that, but I do now, trust me. So while I do want you all with me, I might be asking too much given the circumstances. You do whatever feels right and that'll be good enough for me. No hard feelings." She gave a smile that looked both forced and sad. "But if you decide to come, I want you to be my matron of honor."

Then, with her head high, she walked out the door, leaving Miranda standing there, absorbing the impact of her words, trying to sort through how she felt, how Victoria might feel.

She was still trying when Troy came in.

His expression assured her he'd overheard everything, and a part of her wanted to demand to know why he hadn't shown up to support her, a part that needed someone to blame.

But Troy wasn't at fault here. He'd done exactly what a supportive husband should have done—he'd respected that this had been between her and her sister.

"Do you want to talk about it?" His thoughtful tone proved he knew how rattled she was.

But what was there to talk about? How every decision she made lately seemed to be the wrong one?

Perfect, Victoria had called her, but she felt so far from perfect she could have cried. She *wasn't* going to cry, damn it.

"Not now, thanks."

Then she headed into the bathroom. She was going to take her shower now. *Before* her head exploded. *Before* she dissolved into a puddle of stupid tears that would only convince Troy that he'd married a basket case.

10

TROY HAD WONDERED how he could have been so blind to what was happening in his marriage, but now he had to question his intelligence at how long it had taken him to put two and two together. For the past twenty minutes, he'd sat at the dining room table, listening to a heated exchange carry through the open oasis doors, before finally understanding the problem.

He'd married into a family that didn't have the first clue how to show they cared about each other.

Miranda's family held such rigid ideas about acceptable and unacceptable behavior that they spent more time living up to those ideals than actually living. It was no wonder Miranda spent so much time and energy keeping up appearances.

Marriage isn't just about love. It requires a great deal of work and commitment, her words came back to mind.

Their Web site overflowed with her upbeat reports about the routine tasks he left her to deal with.

He stayed in contact but had wrapped himself in work and left her to keep their lives running smoothly. She'd picked up every ball he had tossed her way and juggled it capably. That was Miranda—a woman used to demanding a lot from herself and usually accomplishing it.

But Troy knew life didn't always run smoothly, and she must have hit some snags along the way. Yet he couldn't remember ever hearing about any. Why? Because Miranda was a woman used to forging ahead with a smile on her face? What happened when she got in over her head?

Suddenly her slow withdrawal made sense. She was struggling with something—not acclimating to their new home, a problem, *something*—working harder and harder to deal with it, not sharing it with him because she knew she only had to keep up appearances until he shipped out again.

And she had every right to feel that way.

What had he ever done to encourage her to ask for help?

Sure, he asked her how things were going at home, but was asking enough for a strong, capable woman like Miranda? And if he'd really been interested in what was happening while he'd been away, would he have accepted her assurances at face value for so long?

Troy wasn't impressed with his answer.

Now he was left to face that his actions weren't enough, not nearly enough, and he didn't see a quick fix. Correcting this problem meant changing his actions, expressing an interest while he was away, making himself more accessible until Miranda felt comfortable opening up to him.

All that would take time, which was the one thing he didn't have right now. He'd pushed her into this investigation, so she was knee-deep in alligators with her family.

He had to help her solve this problem *now*.

Making his way across the room, Troy glanced inside the bedroom to make sure she was still in the shower. Pulling the door shut, he headed to the desk and dialed 1-9 on the house phone.

Laura answered with a pleasant greeting on the second ring and Troy found himself mildly surprised at how quickly he knew what he needed to do. "Have you spoken to Victoria yet?"

"She just left my office after telling me the search is off, the weddings are on, but the ushers will have to seat my guests on both sides of the room because she won't have any."

Troy laughed, encouraged that he could still find humor in this situation. "That about sums it up."

"Isn't there anything we can do?"

He recognized the resolve behind the question and knew that no matter what had happened to split his wife's family from Laura's, these women were all cut from the same strong mold.

"That's what I called about, Laura. How committed are you to getting this family back together?"

"Very."

He fixed his gaze on the closed bedroom door that embodied the distance separating him from Miranda and knew that he faced the fiercest battle ahead.

Clearing away all the obstacles between him and his wife.

"Good, then I'm going to need your help."

MIRANDA STOOD in the shower, willing the jets to soothe away the remnants of her headache. She needed this hot water to pound her thoughts into some manner of calm.

She tried to understand what had led to her confrontation with Victoria, but the only thing she understood was that history was repeating itself.

All because of one man's expectations for his family.

Victoria had accused their grandfather of selfishness, but in her heart she knew there was more, that the problem was bigger than any of them knew. Why else would her grandfather turn his back on his oldest daughter, give up his youngest granddaughter and split their family down the middle?

Why would this man who stood for truth, honesty and the American way lie to her face?

She'd walked into his study to live up to her familial responsibility, but she'd pushed her grandfather into taking action against Victoria instead.

Miranda arched backward beneath the spray, rinsing shampoo from her hair and wishing the water would cleanse away the image of her sister's face in all its reconciled, *hurt* glory.

I've put you all in a tough position. I didn't always understand that, but I do now, trust me, she'd said.

Yes, that was all true, but did Victoria really deserve to be cut out of the family, to plan a wedding believing that her nearest and dearest wouldn't show up?

Despite the pulsing hot water, Miranda shivered. She hadn't done a thing to ease her sister's uncertainty, her hurt, and she couldn't help but wonder if her mother had felt just as hurt when her big sister left the family home and didn't look back.

Did she feel abandoned? Betrayed?

Did Victoria feel that way now?

You're the perfect sister.

Perfect? That was such a joke Miranda might have

laughed—except that there was nothing funny about this situation or the way she felt right now. Or the way Victoria must feel.

As if she wasn't good enough.

After venturing away from her little pond, Miranda had discovered how it felt to not make the cut. She'd learned what it felt like to be excluded, the way Laura had once been excluded at school.

Yet even with these painful lessons under her belt, she'd carelessly fostered the same feeling with her sister.

Victoria was a rebel. She dated unsuitable men. Her idea to get the families back together was risky, crazy.

So many criticisms replayed in her memory. Yet had Miranda ever asked why her sister acted the way she did, why she felt the need to grab life by both hands?

Not once.

In her mind the family expectations had always been clear-cut and simple. She'd done her best to live up to them, and as Carolyn Ford's daughter, she'd had a lot to live up to, knew the pressure firsthand.

How would it feel for Victoria to walk behind her?

You're the perfect sister.

Far from it, but how would Victoria know that she struggled under that same pressure, too? How *could* she know when Miranda had never shared that part of herself?

Not even with her husband.

No, she'd hidden inside this shower when she'd really felt like crying on Troy's shoulder. She'd wanted him to hold her, support her, love her. He wouldn't have passed judgment or said the things she already knew in her heart.

She *should* have handled the situation differently.

She was a *terrible* sister.

He would never blame her for drowning in her troubles with the witchy wives. He wouldn't care that all her grand plans to support his career by making nice on base had blown up in her face. He wouldn't care about anything except that she felt isolated and alone and like a complete failure because she was so affected by these petty women and their nonsense.

And when she thought about that, Miranda remembered that Victoria wasn't the first one to accuse her of perfection.

We can't all endure our lot in life so gracefully, Miranda, a witchy wife had said to her once upon a time. Several others had nodded in agreement. *I'm afraid we're not perfect. We're just normal women who miss our husbands and worry about them coming home safely.*

Miranda remembered her shock at this woman's words. How could she, how could any of them, think that Miranda didn't feel exactly the same way about Troy? But now that she thought about it…when had she ever actually expressed that she felt that way? Had she ever shared her feelings with these women?

No.

She'd sat at the luncheons and teas, chatting about everything under the sun but her feelings. She'd considered those private, had thought admitting she worried about Troy a sign of weakness.

She'd felt that way about the women, too. They'd chosen military life when they'd married their husbands and should buck up and deal with the unique demands. She'd interpreted their commiserating as complaining. Their openness about their worries and fears had made her uncomfortable. Why?

Because she was uncomfortable with her feelings?

Because she thought her worries meant she was weak? Troy was out defending their country while she was drowning in self-doubt because of a bunch of witchy women.

Because listening to other wives voice their worries about their husbands made her worry all the more about Troy?

Or all of the above?

These were questions that needed answers, questions that meant taking a hard look at herself. No, it wouldn't be easy, but when she thought about it, nothing about the past year had been.

Except for loving Troy.

That had been as natural as breathing, the one constant. So hanging on to the thought, Miranda finally left the shower, ready to stop hiding.

She found Troy sitting on the edge of the fountain in the oasis, sipping his coffee and staring into the forest beyond the windows.

She recognized his look, knew he was deep in thought. His hair seemed to glow golden in the morning sun, and she paused in the open doorway to watch him, captured by the sight, by the familiar rush of emotions.

A calm smoothed away the raw edges of her mood and an excitement awoke inside her, a feeling that she stood poised on the brink of her whole life, that each breath would bring a new experience. She knew this feeling, a reaction unique to Troy, one she'd let worries distract her from for too long.

Their together time was precious, and they'd promised each other long ago not to waste a minute. She hadn't been living up to her end of the deal, had been shielding herself behind her doubts. But no more.

With a sense of purpose, she stepped inside, inhaled deeply of the ripe summer scents, and smiled when he glanced up.

His clear gaze swept over her, a look of such yearning that her heart squeezed around a beat. She recognized his frown, the tightening of his jaw, knew he was worried about her.

"I'm ready to talk about Victoria now," she said.

"You okay?"

His tender tone squeezed her heart a little more. "I will be."

"So how are we going to fix this?"

We.

Sitting on the fountain edge beside him, Miranda took his coffee mug and set it aside. She twined her fingers through his, and his grip tightened on hers, his work-roughened hands so strong and capable, if she'd only let him share his strength with her.

And she would. One step at a time. She'd take that first step by opening up about her sister and letting him help her find a resolution.

"I won't sit back and let another generation of sisters be divided," she said.

"Glad to hear it. So what's the plan?"

She shrugged. "I was hoping you'd help me with that."

"Really?" He searched her expression with a stoic gaze. "I thought you'd rather fly solo."

There was a world of implication in those words, yet she sensed no anger or resentment. Only an offer.

"Not *rather.* Just not sure how to do it differently."

Troy seemed to recognize how big this admission was because he scooted closer, rested his forehead against hers. "I'm here."

"I know." Exhaling a soft sigh, she absorbed the promise in his words, a tangible feeling that radiated through her like the warmth of his skin.

It was a thoughtful moment, filled with a tenderness that drove home how she'd closed herself off from these moments, how she'd been distancing herself from the intimacy that was such a special part of their relationship.

There were so many wonderful things about being married to Troy, but she'd allowed herself to get consumed by pressures and worries when she should have been focusing on what they had together.

No more.

And she'd taken the all-important first step.

"We've got some decisions to make," she said, feeling that sense of purpose.

"Yeah, we do."

We.

She wasn't sure what the next step would be, but with Troy's help she'd figure it out.

A smile softened his features, erasing his frown. "So talk, Miranda. Let's tackle the problems so we can get on with our day."

"Ready for a mud bath, are you?"

"I get enough of mud during land maneuvers, so there's been another change in plans."

"Don't tell me you want to go fishing again."

He shook his head. "Something I thought you'd enjoy more."

"You don't think I enjoyed fishing?"

Arching a brow, he stared down at her until she laughed.

"All right, I wouldn't have chosen to go fishing if I'd been choosing, Troy, but honestly, it wasn't as bad as I'd thought."

"Glad to hear it, but you're such an accommodating wife I think you'd make the best out of bootcamp if you thought it would make me happy."

There was *something* in his tone that suggested he wasn't convinced this was such a great thing.

"I like spending time with you. And I don't expect our interests always to run in the same directions. Take right now for example. I'm sure you'd rather get on with our day rather than discuss what to do about my family."

"Furniture shopping was worse."

She laughed, his smile and the bright summer morning acting as a balm for her mood. The lush smells of the blooms. The bubbling rhythm of the fountain. She was on her way to solving the problem and she felt hopeful. "This is supposed to be our fantasy vacation. You haven't been home in so long, you deserve a chance to enjoy yourself, not have to worry about *stuff*."

"That *stuff* is my life, Miranda. I can't stop living it because I'm away. I don't want to. If I haven't made that clear before then give me another chance because I will."

She didn't doubt that he meant what he said. That statement was full of implication, but she wasn't sure what he felt responsible for. "Troy, you haven't done anything you need another chance for—"

"Shh." He pressed a kiss to her lips. "Let's not worry about anything now except how to solve the immediate problem with your family. We'll figure everything else out. Trust me."

"I do."

He sat back with a smile. "Then where do we start?"

"I've messed things up completely by going to my grandfather."

"You did what you thought was best."

"I sold out my sister."

"You couldn't know how the senator would react."

She stared down at their clasped hands, his skin so dark against hers. "No, I couldn't, but I shouldn't have taken the chance. Victoria didn't have much room to play with. I knew that."

"You saw potential risks. It was a no-win situation."

Miranda gazed up into those clear green eyes, saw so much love there, felt the weight of living up to so much love. "Are you going to rationalize everything to make me feel better?"

"I'm not rationalizing. I'm giving you perspective. I do have a plan to make you feel better, but not until we decide what to do about your family."

"What plan?"

"A tension building plan. That's the game, right? Tease and torture to build the tension."

She nodded. "And you scheduled this in place of our mud bath?"

"It's a surprise for later."

"Should I be worried?"

"Later." He kissed her again. "Let's analyze the problem and come up with a way to fix it."

"Plotting a campaign here, Lieutenant Commander?"

"That's what I do." He traced the arch of her brow.

"So the first thing we have to do is establish the goal. What do you want to happen here?"

"We've got to stop history from repeating itself. Not only am I responsible for siccing my grandfather on Victoria, but my mother doesn't need this stress. I can't imagine how she'll feel if Grandfather insists she boycott the wedding."

"Will she?"

"No. I suspect she does miss her sister. She won't give up Victoria the same way, but being forced to stand between two people she loves will devastate her."

"How much time do we have?"

"Victoria told me she'd talk to Laura and call off the search. Then she'll handle grandfather."

"Sounds like the problem's already solved."

She shook her head. "It isn't. Victoria will call off the search to satisfy Grandfather, but that doesn't mean she'll get what she wants."

"Which is?"

She scowled. "The *whole* family together at her double wedding with Laura and Dale."

Troy shook his head as if to clear it. "Whoa, I missed that part."

"She wants both sides of our family to celebrate at the wedding and live happily ever after."

He raised her hands to his lips, brushed his mouth across her knuckles. "This place has gone to her head."

"This place is insane. That's all there is to it."

"Insane, or magic?" He looked so amused, she knew he'd already decided on which it was.

Miranda wished she thought so, too, but from her own struggles with self-doubt and vanishing orgasms to facing a long-term family rift… "Everything *feels* insane."

He reached up to thumb stray hairs from her temple. His skin brushed hers, warm, a tender touch that underscored their closeness, a newfound intimacy. "What do you want to happen?"

Somewhere between the time she'd gotten into the shower and back out again, Miranda had figured out what she wanted. She could answer this question with certainty. "I want the people I love to be happy. I just didn't realize how much I wanted it until seeing Victoria and Laura together. My sister and I have grown too far apart."

He trailed his fingers down her cheek, a thoughtful touch that made her feel wanted, loved, hopeful. "An epiphany. I'll bet you never expected one of those when we checked-in for our stint as the Hottest Honeymoon Couple."

"No, I didn't." She'd expected to leave her problems behind but they'd followed her instead.

Turning her face, she pressed a kiss against Troy's hand, feeling the weight of the burden she'd carried so long unexpectedly lighten enough that she could take a deep breath.

"So how much are you willing to risk to reach mission objective?" he asked.

"You're the big sister, Miranda. It's your job to keep an eye on Victoria, to protect her if she needs protecting."

Victoria needed protecting now.

Miranda's path suddenly appeared crystal clear. *If* she had the guts to take it. Lately, it seemed, every time she took a left turn she should have taken a right. But that was self-doubt talking and she'd already decided to jettison self-doubt.

"As long as Victoria's out of the picture, she's off the hook. What if you and I continue our investigation, figure out what happened thirty years ago and then I talk with my grandfather?"

This time she wouldn't run away from a confrontation.

Troy gave a low whistle. "What makes you think he won't cut *you* off?"

"He might."

"And you're willing to risk this whole situation blowing up in everyone's face?"

"Yes."

"For Victoria?"

"Yes." *Because that's what big sisters did.* "I don't think it will explode in our faces. My grandfather lied to me, Troy. I didn't call him on it because I was afraid it would hurt him."

And she'd been afraid to deal with the way that felt. "But this isn't about me and what I want. Now that he's made a stand, it's about more than just him. It's about Victoria and my mother, too. If we find out what the problem is, I can sit down and rationally discuss what to do about it. All I want is for this family to be together at the wedding and give our mothers a chance to make peace if that's what they want."

"You'll blackmail him?"

"I would *never*." She scowled, not believing he'd spoken the word. "I'll negotiate with the facts. My grandfather can let the past stay in the past so we can have our weddings in peace, or he can choose to drag it all into the present. We'd have done this already if he'd have just answered my question honestly."

"That's blackmail, Miranda."

"It's *negotiation*. My grandfather respects good business. He taught me all about it."

"It's a calculated risk."

No denying that. She inclined her head in agreement.

"Miranda Knight doesn't take calculated risks. I know. I married her."

"It's time for a change."

Troy leaned forward to kiss her, a quick kiss on the edge of a laugh. "Another epiphany?"

"Yes."

11

WHEN A KNOCK SOUNDED at the door, Troy headed across the room, pausing for effect with his hand on the knob. "Are you ready to forget about everything except feeling good for a little while?"

"Is this my surprise?"

"We're going to relax and regroup," he said, cutting off any chance for a reply when he flung the door wide to reveal a smiling Laura.

"Greetings, my Hottest Honeymoon Couple. Are you ready for us?" At Troy's nod, she stepped inside the suite and motioned behind her. "Come on in, everyone."

Troy backed into the living room to make way for the half dozen hotel staff who filed inside the suite behind loaded pushcarts. As they passed, he could make out swaths of faux fur, an array of erotic items from silk restraints to leather paddles and stacks of neatly folded sheets.

Oh, yeah. This was just what the doctor ordered.

Miranda sidled close, her eyes widening as she watched each cart disappear into the bedroom. "What's all this?"

"The make your own sheet set party."

"Wasn't this supposed to happen in the Toy Shoppe?"

"I thought you could use a distraction, Mrs. Knight,

so I had Laura make the party to go. Are you up to being distracted?"

A slow smile touched her mouth. "I think that's exactly what I need."

Troy moved in and twined a silky black curl around his finger, deeply pleased with her reaction. Not only to the sheet set party but to Victoria's visit earlier. Her decision to open up about the problem and involve him in the solution moved them in the direction he wanted to go, and he appreciated this chance to convince her there was magic happening around here.

To convince her to believe in *them.*

He had Miranda's heart, but he wanted more. He wanted her to talk to him, to share her feelings. He wanted to prove to her that he was interested in everything about her, not only the easy, but the tough, too. No distance or war or any *trouble* could come between them if they didn't let it. He didn't think she believed that. Her family had set such a different example. When the going got tough, her family had split ranks.

Leaning toward her, he pressed a kiss to her mouth, felt a sudden rush of longing when her lips parted beneath his. Unable to resist, he speared his fingers into those cool silk curls and guided her head back, drawing her deeper into their kiss. He swept his tongue inside, tasted their desire, hot and needy and sweet, his own raw edged with an urgency that drove home how much rode on making her believe.

When the bedroom door closed, the sound echoed through the suite and dragged them from the moment. He gazed down at his wife, the color riding high in her cheeks, her eyes sparkling with excitement.

"Shouldn't be long," he said.

"I had no idea you were so high maintenance, Lieutenant Commander. Laura must regret sending us an invitation to her grand opening."

"Laura wants to make peace with you for her mother's sake. She's more than willing to do whatever it takes to accommodate us."

Half sitting on the arm of the sofa, he looped his arms loosely around her waist and pulled her toward him. "So let's discuss terms."

"Of what?"

"Tease and Torture. You're in charge. I want to know what'll throw the game."

"When one of us begs, of course."

He'd suspected as much, but had needed to be sure. "You told me this was win-win, Mrs. Knight."

Laughter sparkled in her eyes. To his surprise, and profound pleasure, she leaned forward and pressed her mouth to his cheek. "And it will be, Lieutenant Commander. I'll have a very good time making you beg."

"You think *I'll* be the one to beg first?"

She eyed him boldly. "I had no idea you had such a big ego."

"I'm with the United States Navy, ma'am," he drawled. "Of course I have a big ego."

Tugging her between his legs, he kissed the reply from her lips, coaxing her into one of those soul-deep numbers that made him glad he was sitting. His blood began to slog through his veins, hot and potent, every throb of his pulse swelling with erotic potential. Her breaths filtered across his lips in warm bursts. He traced his tongue along her bottom lip, a moist stroke that made her shiver.

To his profound pleasure, she slipped her hands around his neck and idly toyed with his nape, a teasing touch that aroused places inside him that should have been a lot harder to awaken after nearly three weeks at a romance resort.

When the door cracked open, Miranda sprang back with a laugh, her chest rising and falling on shallow breaths. He'd play her game as long as she wanted him to, but he wanted a chance to convince her that she didn't want to keep playing. "Your game seems to be working. The tension's already building."

She only nodded, and then Laura's entourage emerged from the bedroom with empty pushcarts. Troy held the door wide as they proceeded across the suite in single file.

"Have fun," Laura said. "I'm 1-9 on the house phone if you need anything else."

And Troy wouldn't hesitate to call if he did. Laura had proven herself an unexpected and valuable ally, and he thanked her while escorting her to the door. Giving them a conspiratorial wink, she slipped out behind her staff.

"You are not going to believe this," Miranda said.

With a smile at her breathless tone, he turned to find her standing inside the bedroom. He joined her, gazing into the once-familiar room that had been transformed into a fantasy.

With its shimmering fabric draped from the ceilings and the bright gold furnishings, the Egyptian Pleasure Pyramid was exotic on a normal day, but what Laura and her staff had created in a short period of time was beyond exotic.

The bed had been stripped except for a white silk

cover encasing the mattress. A portable shelf displayed
an array of sheet sets in a variety of fabrics and colors.
Each set sat in a neatly folded pile with a corner draped
outward, an artful trick that seemed the hallmark of
five-star hotels. Blushing pink. Brazen black. Tempting
tan. A palette of colors for any mood.

Glancing at his wife, Troy found her darting her gaze
between tables that had been set up in every free area
in the room. Covered in rich velvet display cloths, each
held a variety of items. From this vantage he could
make out bottles of lotions and sex toys. A table for restraints. One devoted to protection.

His blood began to pulse warm and thick through his
veins and he looped his arm through hers and asked,
"Shall we?"

Inclining her head, she let him lead her farther inside
and he could sense her excitement in the way she held
herself as they strolled toward the first table.

"How does she do this?" Miranda reached for a
brightly colored cellophane package.

"Do what?"

"*This.*" She waved the package around, motioning
around the room. "She turns everything into a fantasy
and this room was a fantasy already."

"I know you and Laura have a past, but would I hurt
your feelings if I said she's gifted?"

Miranda met his gaze and smiled. "Once upon a time
you would have, but not anymore. I think Laura was on
target when she said we've all behaved toward each other
the way we'd been expected to behave. I don't really know
her. I never did. If she has a gift for creating fantasies, then
I'll just be grateful she's sharing that gift with us."

After all the revelations on this visit home, Troy understood enough about her history with Laura to recognize what an admission this was for Miranda.

"Me, too." Lifting her hand to his mouth, he pressed a kiss to her knuckles, tasted the smooth skin there. "So here we are in a room filled with sex toys. Are you still so sure I'll be the one begging?"

"Mmm-hmm."

"You do realize you're challenging me."

"Mmm-hmm." She stepped toward him, spanning the mere inches between them. His bold wife knew just what he wanted then. He recognized the flare of desire in her eyes, sensed in that moment that he'd accomplished mission objective by distracting her big-time.

There was nothing between them except a growing erotic challenge. She wanted him to beg. He wanted her to beg. It was a potent combination. And with the variety of sex toys around them, he thought they both stood a good chance of getting what they wanted.

Miranda slipped out of his arms in a playful move, leaving him feeling the sudden distance between them, but he didn't complain. Not when she swept her curly mane over her shoulder and reached for her zipper.

Troy braced himself for the show he sensed was about to begin, and Miranda didn't disappoint him. She walked away with graceful strides, her bottom swaying gently. She treated him to the sight of her creamy skin as her summer dress parted then glided down her body bit by luscious bit.

She'd dressed for a trip to the spa and their scheduled visit to the mud baths. Her dress was the easy-on-easy-off kind, and she wore no hose. So when the dress

slithered into a puddle at her feet, she stood there i
nothing more than a bra, thong and sandals, all gorgeou
legs and sleek skin.

Until she stepped out of the circle of fabric, an
leaned over to grab her dress.

His chest constricted around a breath as she bent ove
giving him a glimpse of her heart-shaped bottom in a
its curvy glory, her cheeks parting just enough to sho
him where that skinny silk strap of her thong was hidin

She'd been married to him long enough to kno
what the sight of her like this would do to him. Bloo
surged so hard to his crotch that he felt dizzy.

Bracing himself against the table, Troy sucked in
deep breath, realizing how much trouble he was in an
they hadn't even gotten the first sheet on the bed.

He reminded himself *she* would be the one beggin
today.

"This is torture, Mrs. Knight." The words scrape
through his throat, proving he needed the reminder.

"You want to see me naked, and I want to feel thos
sheets against my skin. That's the only way I can te
which ones to put on the bed."

"Who knew housekeeping could be so erotic?" No
him for sure. "We need to remember this. If you'r
naked, I'll bet I won't mind furniture shopping so much

She chuckled and stood upright, a liquid motion tha
made her hair swing down her back in a fall of gloss
curls. "They'll have to deliver the furniture to the hous
because I won't be undressing in the showroom."

"Not ready to explore an exhibition fetish?"

"Nope. But I'm game to try out a few other fetishe
while we have a private room filled with them."

"Do you know you made me the happiest man alive on our wedding day?"

Her expression told him she'd needed the reassurance and took his words to heart. It vanished almost as quickly as it had come, and she flashed him a sultry smile.

And unhooked her bra.

He could see the full swell of breast as the white satin rode up, teasing him with visions of what her blushing nipples would look like if the fabric rode up just a little more.

And it did. When she leaned over a table to inspect a table filled with bottles, tubes and jars, she revealed even more of her breast in profile, just enough of the creamy shape to tease him, the gesture seeming wildly erotic.

"I've never seen so much...*stuff*." She stood again holding a bottle up for his perusal. "Pleasure and Sizzle, a naughty nipple cream. Coochie Coo Shaving Gel, this one's self-explanatory. Peter Butter? Can you imagine working for the companies that have to advertise this stuff? An interesting day on the job, I'd guess." She chuckled. "Oh, here's one. Happy Penis Lotion, an edible penis sensitizer. Oh, Lieutenant Commander, I bet you'd like that."

"I don't need to be any more sensitive right now." She was trying to tip the scales in her favor, but she wasn't going to find him such an easy mark.

If he could get a few brain cells functioning. Just the sight of Miranda in those strappy high heels with her legs silky and bare made it hard to think straight.

His erection had grown rock hard, despite the seam cutting into his skin. He should loosen his pants—but

with his blood pounding so hard, he thought it migh
hurt more to move.

So he stayed put while Miranda cracked open the li
of a bottle and lifted it to her nose for a whiff.

"Oh, I might like this one. 'An edible stimulant in
delicious mango flavor,'" she read from the packaging
"You like fruit for breakfast." Dabbing some on her fin
ger, she brought it to her lips, leaving Troy to fixate o
the way her pink tongue darted out for a taste.

"Mmm." She sucked her finger inside, mouth pursed
eyes smiling as she mimed an erotic motion that mad
him ache.

Teasing him further, she withdrew her finger an
held it up so he could see the moisture glistening on he
skin. "Tasty. I wonder if this stuff works." She shot hin
a bold look from beneath her lashes. "Only one way t
find out."

And as Troy stood there, heart pounding so loud h
thought his ears would explode, his crotch painfully test
ing the seam of his pants, she dribbled more on her finge
and began an erotic dance of fingers over her skin…down
down, *down* toward the skimpy V of her thong.

Her fingers disappeared beneath that scrap of silk an
Troy stood transfixed as she touched herself, lingerin
caresses that made his chest constrict.

"It's slick." She sounded thoughtful, and her hai
swung forward to cover her face as she glanced be
tween her thighs.

He thought about joining her, about forcing his leg
to move so he could feel some skin and ease this ache
but he wouldn't stop this show. Not when Miranda ha
let her hair down in a big way and he had a glimpse o

the woman he hadn't seen in so long, the woman who'd withdrawn too far inside herself, the woman he wouldn't let get away.

"I think it's getting warmer." She sucked in a hissing breath. "*Definitely* warmer."

She rolled her finger around again, her mouth pursed around the sound of an "Oh!" He watched her knead that inviting place between her legs, her hips gently arching into each touch. He knew she'd caught a good spot because she made a sound that was half laugh, half gasp and lifted her gaze to his.

He recognized the surprised pleasure in her expression and couldn't wipe away his own stupid smile when her loose bra rode up just enough so a breast popped out.

He finally got to see some nipple, the blushing peak puckered and tight as her breast swayed heavily with the motion. She was a vision with her hair curling behind her shoulders as she let her head drop back, her throat arching toward him, her body all sleek curves, one breast peeking out to tempt him, the other still hidden precariously in her bra.

Miranda seemed determined to torture him as she played with herself, lazy circles that were making her skin flush—a sight that was damn near crippling him with arousal.

"The tension's building," Troy ground out, his admission making her smile.

"Is it?"

He was gratified, and relieved, that she sounded nearly as needy. "I don't think I've ever been this hot for you."

And that was saying a lot.

Miranda obviously knew it, too, because she slid her hand from her panties, her fingers leaving a trail of moisture along her smooth skin.

"Shall we get on with our choosing then?"

"I can't move," he admitted.

Her eyes popped open and she looked at him. "Why not?"

"My dick is so hard it'll break."

With a laugh, she pushed away from the table and made a move toward him. "My poor husband."

He held out his hand. "Don't come any closer or I'm going to attack you right now and lose this game."

She sidestepped him, and moved just out of reach, sliding the bra down her arms. "That's exactly what I want, Lieutenant Commander. Just let go. I'll satisfy you."

His few working brain cells registered that she didn't agree to make love to him. She'd *satisfy* him. And that served as enough of a reminder to reclaim a little of his control. Forcing himself to move, he suffered the pressure from that damned seam.

She sent the bra whizzing past his head. It landed on the table behind him, spread out over packages of Incredible Edibles.

"Do you really think you can resist, Lieutenant Commander?"

Not if she kept firing salvos like this, and he didn't even mind. "Oh, I can resist. Want to up the stakes and bet me?"

She considered him thoughtfully, and he liked the way she rose to his challenge, clearly empowered by her desire and her certainty that she'd win this bet. "Okay, but let's wager something good. Why don't we play Chain of Command? The winner gets to be in charge."

This was a game they'd played before, and a rather fond memory of a time he'd arrived home from duty to find Miranda stretched out on their new couch wearing nothing but his dress hat and a salute replayed in his mind to torture him some more.

She'd been in command that time, and the memory nearly made his brain melt.

"Just think about being in command of all these sexy goodies." She swept her hand around the room. "I've already seen some things I'd command you to use."

"Really? Like what."

With a few slinky strides, she headed toward a table that housed a variety of dildos and vibrators, including the dual temperature number.

Locating a small golden one from the table, she held it up. Not much more than three inches tall, it seemed rather innocuous from where he stood.

"You want me to use that on you?" he asked.

Turning the dildo in her hand, she considered it carefully. "This is the Plug of Kings. I want to use it on *you*."

Damned if he didn't realize exactly what that *innocuous* looking thing was just then, and there was nothing innocuous about where she wanted to stick it.

"I've always thought of myself as an accommodating husband," he said, sobering up a bit. "Guess I was wrong."

With a laugh, she replaced the offensive device back on the table. "If you win, you'll get to pick. Unless you're squeamish? Would you rather bet something else?"

At the moment Miranda stood a much better chance of outlasting him, and he'd wind up finding out what it felt like to be on the receiving end of a sex toy he'd rather not make the acquaintance of.

So he didn't answer, just watched her pause in front of the sheets to finger the various fabrics. He finally forced himself to move, willing the activity to lessen the physical effects of his nearly naked wife. Sidestepping her, he flung open the doors to the oasis, filling the room with the bubbling sounds of water, the smooth strains of exotic music.

Inhaling the scented air, he commanded his body to relax—no easy job with Miranda still putting on a show.

And this was a show designed to bring him to his knees. He watched as she lifted the corner of a shiny pink sheet and dragged it along her arm, testing the fabric against her skin.

Then she unfolded a sheet that looked like a faux version of a bearskin rug, bundled it against her, and buried her breasts in the plush faux fur.

And made his crotch ache in the process.

A condition he'd willingly endure. Miranda was finally venturing out from behind her careful persona and that was exactly what he wanted. He'd missed her, but he'd never realized how much until he saw her relaxed again.

"Like that one?" He could be an accommodating husband after all. So when she lifted her blue gaze to his and nodded, he said, "I'll take your bet. No sweat."

"Unless I win, hmm?" She sounded sassy.

"I can handle whatever you have in mind."

No question. There wasn't anything he'd rather do than help his beautiful wife learn to believe in how good they were together.

And besides, Troy planned to win. He'd been maneuvering behind Miranda's back, with his mom and Laura, and he wasn't crazy enough to forget it. When she found out, it wouldn't hurt him to have some leverage.

Now, he just had to control himself.

12

"YOU CAN HANDLE WHATEVER I have in mind, Lieutenant Commander?" Miranda asked. "Even the Plug of Kings?"

She wanted to know. She needed to know. She wasn't ready to give up the control of her game yet. And with that thought, the heat of her arousal drained away, leaving her standing there feeling naked and cold.

And thinking, damn it.

Sheer stubbornness made her unfold the Polar Bear Pack sheet set, snuggle against the pristine faux fur and close her eyes. She'd taken her first step today toward changing the things that weren't working for her, and that change felt positive, empowering. She wasn't running or hiding from her emotions anymore. She would face the consequences of her choices, face her grandfather, to get what she considered important in life—being close to her husband and her family.

Witchy wives meant nothing. When she got down to it, confrontations, public opinion and long-term family rifts didn't matter much, either.

Her handsome husband and her family *did*.

She wasn't running and hiding from vanishing orgasms, either. She refused to let doubts and uncertainty spoil her foreplay, too. She wouldn't try to distract Troy. She wouldn't back down from this problem again.

Not *ever*.

If another orgasm vanished, she wouldn't feel bad about herself, wouldn't let it become a big deal. Yes, it was another calculated risk, but one she would willingly take. After the way Troy had looked at the Plug of Kings, she knew he had a lot more at stake right now than she did.

"So what gives?" she asked, pleased to sound so confident, so in control. "I thought you weren't crazy about my choice of sex toys?"

Glancing up, she expected to find him still standing in the doorway to the oasis, but suddenly he was behind her, his hands slipping around her, anchoring her against him.

"Troy!" She gave a breathless laugh as his hard body surrounded her, all lean muscle and powerful male, a rock-hard erection nestling against her lower back. He cradled her against him, buried his face in her hair.

Then he threaded strong fingers along her ribs as he reached up to cup her breasts, and Miranda shuddered at his touch, the way he weighed their fullness with oh-so-erotic care.

Heat spiraled inside, white-hot tendrils that warmed her, chasing away her chill until it was no more than a memory to be brushed aside. Rising up on tiptoes, she pressed herself further into his hands, rocked back against him.

"I plan to win our bet," he told her.

Reaching her hand between them, she slid her fingers over that impressive bulge and gave a meaningful squeeze, and was rewarded when he pressed against her hungrily. "Me, too."

"I won't make love to you until you beg me, Miranda."

His confidence challenged her. "You sound pretty sure for a man with *this* in his pants."

"I am." He swirled his tongue into the shell of her ear, one hot stroke that trickled deep into all her needy places.

She could feel him *everywhere*. His hard thighs braced behind hers. His broad chest a haven to sink back into as he fondled her breasts with idle strokes that made her content to stand here all day.

"This is your game, remember?" he said.

Oh, she remembered all right. Whether he teased or tortured, her tension was building, until his most glancing touches flared her need like wildfire. She felt more challenged than she ever had, eager to meet her handsome husband move for sexy move, to prove she could give as good as she got.

She liked this feeling of abandon when she shed the weight of her worries, when she let herself act without censoring her every move and its potential consequence. And what better place to explore this phenomenon than in Troy's arms?

Miranda couldn't think of any better place, and when he ground that erection between her cheeks again and gave a groan of a dying man, she smiled, deciding to bring her handsome husband to his figurative knees in bed.

They'd see who would be reduced to begging.

Arching her back, she leaned into the stroke, riding that bump so hard she could feel it swell through his pants. But her triumph was short-lived because without warning, his fingers slipped from beneath her breasts to pluck at her nipples.

Fire jolted through her, and she nearly lost her grip on the faux fur sheet.

"You like that," he said.

The question didn't need an answer because Troy knew she did. She exhaled a gasp. Her nipples speared greedily toward his fingers. Her hips rocked against him instinctively, seeking the friction to feed this ache inside.

Here was one of those times when Troy knew her body better than she did herself. He added his kisses to the game, kept up that steady tweaking and twisting that overrode any desire to stay cool and not let him see how much he affected her.

Holding up the Polar Bear Pack sheets, Miranda willed herself to relax, stepped away and turned around to face him. "I choose these."

He peered down at her with those striking green eyes, a gaze that became a caress. The sheets flowed to the floor, partially covering her, yet even so, her thong and sandals felt like nothing beneath the hunger flaring in his expression, the loving tenderness in his eyes. She felt naked before his fully clothed self, naked and oh-so loved.

With a nod, he reached out to take a sheet from her and said, "Allow me."

Heading toward the bed, he shook out the sheet as he went, leaving Miranda to watch him, to inhale a deep, relieved breath as she segued through the tense moment, and focused her thoughts back where they belonged right now.

On the man who was making the bed with the sharp easy moves he'd honed during years in the Navy.

"Where'd you learn to make a bed like that?" she

asked, a familiar question that had turned into a joke through the years.

Tossing a grin over his shoulder, he gave her the answer she'd come to expect. "You should appreciate a man who can make a better bed than you do."

"Oh, I do, Lieutenant Commander. I do."

Her admission was rich with implication because in that moment Miranda had never felt luckier.

Like the specialty sheet sets that housekeeping had supplied daily since their arrival at Falling Inn Bed, the Polar Bear Pack had pockets all around the fitted sheet for easy access. The design your own sheet set party meant their job was to fill the pockets.

Glancing around at the variety of sex toys at their disposal, Miranda chose his and hers items from the Incredible Edible table then moved to the table with the lubricants and creams to inspect the offerings there.

Happy Penis Lotion definitely. Troy had earned a happy penis with the thoughtful way he'd let her take the lead without questions. He looked so scrumptious as he leaned over the bed, his pants molding his tight butt, that she felt her arousal reawaken with one moist clench between her thighs.

She'd let him choose the vibrator or dildo himself.

He'd earned that right, too.

Turning back around, he found her smiling at him as he strode toward her, all expectant male. He plucked the goodies from her arms and tossed them onto the bed.

"You, on the bed, while I grab a few things." His words were a command, even though he hadn't won their bet yet.

Miranda wondered what he would choose and draped the flat sheet over the bedpost. Slipping off her sandals, she climbed onto the bed. An interesting match with the huge gold sleigh bed, the faux fur sheets felt as sleek as cool water against her bare skin. Slithering onto her belly, she leaned over the side and fitted her sexy goodies into the sheets pockets.

"Oh, yeah, I like this," Troy said.

She turned to find him watching her while he dangled a chain from his finger. She recognized the padded clamps on the ends and knew where he wanted to attach those clamps.

"Am I in trouble?" she asked.

"Definite trouble."

She felt a thrill of arousal at his tone, a tone that reminded her of his earlier words.

"I won't make love to you until you beg me."

She loved this challenge growing between them, loved that she could escape into this moment and indulge herself. This was the beauty of being married, of feeling so comfortable together that they could share adventures between the sheets.

Dangling the chain from his finger, he strode toward the bed, eyeing her with cool purpose. Her breasts began to tighten at the promise in his expression, a result of the hunger that had been allowed to go unsatisfied. Her head might be racing lately but her body responded to this man on an elemental level, and the design your own sheet set party spread all around them…

She rose to her knees on the edge of the bed, feeling decadent as he towered above her. Reaching out, he brushed his fingers along her cheek.

"Do you mind?" His question filtered between them in the bubbling quiet, erotic, filled with promise.

She shook her head. Her hair cascaded over her shoulders with the motion and the intensity of the moment built until she was aware of the strands against her bare skin.

Troy stepped closer and she expected to feel his hands on her. Indeed, her breasts grew heavy and tight, anticipating his touch. But he lowered his face and zeroed in on a nipple, catching the peak between his lips and drawing her inside with a slow, wet pull.

The shock of his touch reverberated through her like an electrical current, and Miranda reached out to steady herself, gazing down at the top of his blond head. The muscles in his neck flexed and his jaw tensed as he flicked that wicked tongue over the achy peak, and he dragged the cold chain along her stomach, a deliberate, tantalizing move that made her steel herself against the anticipation of what would come next.

With a final swirl of his tongue, he reared back to blow on her nipple, a gust of warm air that somehow felt tender, thoughtful. Then he fitted the clamp around her swollen nipple, and Miranda held her breath as he eased it shut by slow degrees.

A shock wave of sensation made her gasp aloud, the feeling so intense, so potent, she gazed up to find him watching her, gauging her reaction, clearly aroused by the sight.

"Too much?" he asked.

"No." Already the intensity was leveling off to a steady buzz of sensation that made her blood hum. "It's fine."

It was more than fine. They'd never played with this toy before, and the steady pressure echoed through her body, made her feel hypersensitive and excited.

Miranda arched her back and thrust her breasts out. "Go ahead and put that one on."

He gave a husky laugh. "Fine, hmm?"

"*Really* fine." So fine that the erotic pinch was making desire pool low in her belly.

She could almost feel his warm mouth on her skin but this time he thumbed her nipple to life, squeezing it between his fingers, his gaze fixed on her as she gasped out in pleasure.

He fitted the second clamp into place. Another shock wave. Only the weight of the dangling chain intensified the sensation. Her breasts had always been erogenous zones, and Troy skilled in bringing her pleasure with his touches. But this, *this* was enough to make her squirm.

And the man hadn't taken off a stitch of clothing yet.

Her chances of winning this bet were looking slimmer and slimmer by the moment, and that thought had her reaching out for his belt. "I want to feel skin, Lieutenant Commander."

His only response was a light tug on the chain.

The clamps stretched her nipples enough to skyrocket the fever in her blood, one sharp pull that made her cry out, a broken half-gasp, half-moan. The intense sensation shimmered through her entire body, along every nerve ending until her sex clenched hotly and her legs felt weak.

She dragged in another breath, managing her reaction, the need to be touched that was making her ache.

"I like your game, Mrs. Knight," he said. "I like teasing and torturing you."

Before she realized what he was about, he speared his fingers into her hair, forced her head back and lowered his mouth to hers for a hungry kiss.

Their lips collided in a clash of heat, and Mirand[
recognized this phenomenon, this urgent, pressing pa
sion that grew dark. Gone was the easy comfort of
couple who lived together and loved a lot. That comfor
able couple was replaced with two people who kne
each other well enough to push the boundaries, to allo
their hungers to take control, to reveal their deepest d
sires without the fear of reproach.

Troy knew she could handle whatever he tossed
her, just like she knew he'd follow wherever she le
Even if she wanted to build his tension and leave hi
unsatisfied with her game of never-ending torture. The
had trust and respect, and that made this dark, hung
mood all the more titillating.

He drove his tongue deep inside her mouth, his ki
demanding an honest response. Until that moment, sh
hadn't realized how much she'd been holding bac
shielding herself, censuring her reactions, the anticipatic
of a vanishing orgasm preying on the back of her min

Never again.

Miranda threaded her fingers around his head, dre
him deeper into their kiss, an unspoken promise. The
tongues tangled together, and the need swelled betwee
them, impossibly hot, the most wicked of indulgence

His mouth never let up the demand as he trailed
hand down her throat, a forceful touch that left fire i
its wake. When he tugged on the chain again, she crie
out. He captured the sound with his mouth, a possessiv
but tender kiss that pushed her to the edge and cha
lenged her, cherished her.

A kiss that left no room for doubt.

A kiss that convinced her never to hold back from th

special passion they shared, never to hide or retreat or shield herself from a feeling so unique, so extraordinary.

Suddenly she felt Troy's muscles gather and he broke their kiss while locking his fingers into her thong. One tug, and he dragged the silky panties almost to her knees.

"I'll get naked and join you."

She'd wanted to undress him herself, but he'd already backed away from the bed, acting as if he'd won this bet. His tone smacked of his officer's right to command, and after she'd teased him with her own strip-tease, Miranda didn't mind. Not when he had such a wolfish look about him.

She knew this mood, knew his tension mounted in pace with her own. And that was exactly what she wanted right now. Anticipation. Excitement. A good kind of trouble.

She got it in spades when she rolled to her side to remove her panties. The chain swung wildly between her breasts so the clamps tugged on her nipples. The sensation shot through her fast and hard, made her insides melt into a puddle of desire.

And before she'd managed that feeling, Troy's hand connected with her bottom, one sharp slap that made her yelp. He laughed as she swung around to face him, her skin prickling hotly, and her sex growing oh-so wet.

With her heartbeat throbbing in her ears, she stared up at him, found him watching her as if she'd been spread out before him for his pleasure, a tasty morsel to be savored.

He held out a cellophane package.

"Put these on." Another command.

With her bottom tingling hot and that look on his face promising so much pleasure, Miranda took the package.

Incredible Edible Panties.

"I'm going to lick them off you," he said.

"*If* I let you, Lieutenant Commander. You haven
won this bet yet."

He shot her a look of pure sex. "I'll make it wor
your time."

"We'll see." Pure bravado.

"Yes, we will," he promised. "You'll comply or I'
hold you down and spank you some more. I'm bigg
than you."

She rolled to her knees, the chain hanging from h
breasts and weighing on her nipples until she could fe
the ache straight to her toes. But two could play th
game, and she poised her backside high in the air, shoo
ing her husband a suggestive pose that made a flus
creep into his cheeks and his features sharpen wit
barely restrained desire.

"Are you trying to scare me?" she asked.

Troy laughed, another sound she recognized as th
bravado it was because he couldn't resist reaching o
to touch her.

Trailing his hand over the curve of her cheek, h
seemed to be absorbing the heat that still radiated fro
that tender place. They'd played this spanking gam
before, and the exquisite heat of a few well-placed slap
had always given her some seriously memorable o
gasms that *still* had the ability to make her insides me
by just thinking about them.

Troy had been on the reciprocating end before, to
His tight butt made an excellent target, and the revere
way he touched her assured her he was remembering

"You should be scared." His voice was throaty lo

"I'm so horny right now, I don't know if I can control myself."

"Who wants you to control yourself, Lieutenant Commander?"

Certainly not her. She was so hot right now she didn't think this heat would vanish anytime soon. Not when she couldn't think about anything except how hungry her handsome husband looked.

So arching her bottom higher, she rocked her hips to caress the palm he still held against her skin.

Troy smoothed his palm along the curve of her cheek then down her thigh. He brought his hand back up again and grazed her exposed sex, trailing his fingers through the moist folds.

Miranda shivered.

"Do you know what happens when I'm away," he said in an achingly soft voice.

"What?"

"I can get so damn busy I don't have much of a chance to think about everything I'm missing at home. But then you'll launch a new page to our Web site, and I log on to see your picture and read your posts. And I want you, Miranda."

His fingers trailed inside her, just deep enough to tease and torture. His gaze raked over her with aching softness, a look that underscored the conviction in his words.

"Sometimes I want you so bad I'm not sure I'll make it until I get home again. And that want just keeps building until I think I'm going to explode. It's agony."

A slow smile touched his lips. "But I can close my eyes and see you. I can remember what you feel like

when I hold you and how I feel when I'm inside you.
can hear all those little sounds you make, the purrin
sighs and the moans. And I know if I can just hang c
a while longer, that I'll get home and you'll make m
feel that way again. And when I get home, you do."

The longing in his voice crumbled away the edges c
her heart, made her eyes sting with unshed tears. Sh
knew the feeling because she'd felt it herself, only ur
like her, Troy didn't shield himself from the ache or tr
to distract himself. He embraced the way he wanted he
welcomed it.

And she realized just then why their homecoming
were always so overwhelming. Troy's tension ha
mounted to the breaking point, while she'd withdraw
so far inside herself to hide from her longing that sh
needed time to warm up.

Another epiphany.

"I love you," she said.

"I know." He looked at her, his expression hear
achingly gentle. "That's what gets me through—know
ing the reality of being with you will beat the fantas
hands down."

"Always?"

His expression softened and the love in his eyes mad
her heart melt. "Man, it just keeps getting better."

Propping a knee onto the bed, he leaned toward he
swept aside the hair that cascaded all around her, so h
could meet her gaze. "I say thanks every day for yo
Miranda."

"I like the sound of that." More false bravado sh
knew he'd never buy when her voice sounded trembl
and overwhelmed.

"I hoped you would." Then he popped her other cheek, a heated slap that broke the moment. "Now put those on. I'm ready for breakfast."

With a laugh, Miranda rolled away and got to business, treated him to a very deliberate striptease as she kicked off her thong and maneuvered into the pair of nearly see-through blue candy panties.

Blueberry Bonanza.

"You'd better get busy, Lieutenant Commander. I'd hate to melt all over these pretty white sheets."

Troy shoved his slacks over his hips and let them drop to the floor. The fact that he didn't pick them up and fold them away with his usual neatness told her everything she needed to know about his lust level.

"Pleased to know you're hot enough to melt."

"Oh, I am that," she said, and she meant it.

As she stretched out on the furry sheets, watching Troy pull off his socks and hop onto the bed to join her, she not only felt hot and decadent, she felt *excited*. To feel his hands and mouth on her intimate places. And when he clamped his hands around her calves and shimmied her toward him, she let her legs part wide in welcome.

But it wasn't until Troy had licked away every last bite of the edible undies and curled her into the shelter of his hard body to torture her with his sex toy of choice—a wicked little vibrator called the *Extreme-inator*—that Miranda began to appreciate the irony of the situation.

Her husband was on a mission to make her beg, and with an almost supernatural precision, he manipulated that fierce little vibrator into every sensitive place between her thighs.

She kept expecting her thoughts to start racing and chase away another perfectly good orgasm, but the only thing that vanished was her chances of winning this bet.

And that made them both winners in Miranda's book.

She didn't beg exactly, but she did need to climax, and she wanted Troy inside her while she did.

He only wielded that wicked vibration like a weapon, pitching her into a gasping orgasm that proved to be one of those all-over numbers that almost made her swoon…

She could barely keep her eyes open as her trium-phant—*obnoxious?*—husband watched her go to pieces in his arms, the sounds of her moans echoing in the fountain-soaked quiet.

And when she finally managed to catch her breath, she asked, "I cried uncle and you won. Why can't we make love, so I can satisfy you, too?"

He arched a dark brow in a too-smug expression, re-leased her aching nipples from the clamps and told her, "Because I won. Now I get to choose the time and the place."

Miranda heard the threat in there and shivered.

13

Troy HALF SAT on the desk beside Miranda, who sat in front of the computer, still looking soft around the edges after losing their bet. But those dreamy edges were fast giving way to tension as she stared down at the blank monitor.

She lifted her deep gaze to him. "Here to gloat?"

"Nothing to gloat about. We've got a win-win situation."

Definitely win-win. After bringing her to climax with the vibrator, Troy had gone to work on her with the tingly body butter, massaging her delicious curves as if he could speed up the demise of walls that were finally crumbling between them.

After he'd stimulated every inch of her skin had come the Ticklers—a variety of feathers he'd used to tease her sensitive skin until she'd cried uncle again.

"Why didn't we make love so you could claim your prize?"

"I wasn't done teasing and torturing you. Just because I won the bet doesn't mean your game has to be over. It only means I'm in control now." Wrapping his finger in a springy black curl, he tugged, liking the cool silk feel against his skin. "And let's face it, Miranda. I totaled you. I don't make love to comatose women."

"Arrogant man." She gave a haughty sniff. "Doesn't the Navy expect you to be gracious on the field of victory?"

Her body and her orgasms might have been a field of victory today, but only temporarily. He'd won the battle, true, but until Miranda opened up and shared her feelings with him, he hadn't won this war.

Until he understood what had prompted her game of endless foreplay, he wouldn't make love to her. No matter how much he ached to.

And he ached, big-time.

"I won," he said with a shrug. "I get to choose the time and the place."

"Should I be scared?"

"I didn't threaten to treat you like a *king*."

"Had you worried there, hmm?"

He shrugged, still not sure she'd been bluffing. "Would you have really brought that *thing* to bed if you'd won?"

"Only if it would bring you pleasure." Her eyes sparkled, a striking contrast to her creamy skin and glossy hair. "Would you *let* me bring it to bed?"

"If it would bring you pleasure."

Turning her face, she pressed her mouth to his wrist, a gentle kiss that made his blood sizzle. "So you are an accommodating husband."

"I've got a long way to go to live up to my accommodating wife."

The expression softening her features reassured him he would ultimately win this war. And when he did, Troy would claim the spoils on her gorgeous field of victory.

He still had a few weapons tucked away inside the Polar Bear Pack pockets. Some thick velvet ropes to tie her up with...or maybe he should let her tie him up. Miranda enjoyed being in charge, too, and he was so horny now, he'd need restraints to keep his hands off her.

Oh, he looked forward to savoring his victory.

"So, Mrs. Knight. Why are you sitting here staring at a blank computer screen?"

"I can't seem to make myself boot the computer."

"Time to put your money where your mouth is, hmm?"

"It's harder than I thought it would be." She stared up at him, frowning. "I'm having second thoughts about whether or not we're doing the right thing."

"Worried about what you might find?"

She nodded. "Whatever my grandfather is hiding must be big. He'd never keep a secret otherwise. Do I really want to know, let alone be responsible for the possible consequences? That didn't seem to bother Victoria and Laura. It bothers me. A lot."

"The risks aside, they only wanted to find out so they knew how to handle your mothers. If you think you can reason with your grandfather and get him to cooperate without knowing what happened, then go for it." Brushing the glossy curls behind her shoulder, he leaned back and folded his arms across his chest. "It all boils down to mission objective. If you're content with your parents showing up for Victoria's wedding then let's drop the search."

"That's the problem, Troy. In her column tomorrow, Victoria will announce her plans for the double wedding. We're talking major uproar here. Grandfather has already made a stand with her. She's agreed to stop searching but she still won't get what she wants."

"The family back together."

Miranda nodded. "I understand where she's coming from. She wants our mother to have her sister back in her life so she can go off to Vegas and not feel like she's abandoning Mother."

"It's not that much to ask, you know."

"No, not for a normal family, I suppose."

He'd been the one to point that out. "So, we're back to mission objective."

The shadows he saw in her sapphire gaze made him want to wipe her aches away, make her smile. "My grandfather lied to me. How do I know that Victoria wouldn't have gotten what she wanted if I'd have backed her up instead of going to him?"

"History. You did what you thought was best and in all fairness, it really was the sanest thing to do."

"Sane doesn't seem to be on the schedule around this place," she said dryly. "Laura's serving up magic and miracles, and Victoria's jumped on for the ride."

He didn't hear censure in her voice, just irony. That, at least, was a step in the right direction. "I think Laura's been accomplishing some of both. Perhaps she can deliver some more."

"Here's hoping. Once Victoria runs her column, this whole situation is bound to change. People around here lap up any mention of the Fords and the Grangers. Grandfather won't be happy, and Victoria knows it. She's backing him into a corner."

"Then she must be willing to live with the consequences."

Miranda nodded. "She's already reconciled herself to spending her wedding day feeling guilty for making this family rift even worse."

"So what are we going to do? I'm with you no matter what."

"I know," she said softly.

He recognized the way she steeled herself to commit to a course, seemed to draw strength from his presence. He liked that she'd shared her second thoughts with him, too. She was opening up and that was all he wanted. To be included in the process. To get a chance to support her the way she always supported him.

Troy knew the moment she made her decision. She inhaled deeply and her face etched in steely determination.

"Let's do it." She reached down to press the computer's power button. "My sister's wedding is in our hands, and we're going to look out for her."

We.

Hearing that one word tumble from her luscious lips made this unsatisfied ache in his crotch worth every ounce of his restraint. He knew reaching this decision hadn't been easy.

"We will," he said simply.

She replied by reaching to touch his arm, a simple touch that spanned the distance better than words ever could.

"Thank you for helping me. Not just for digging up information on my grandfather but for abandoning me with Victoria earlier."

"Abandoning you?" He scowled. "I was right outside the door. You'd have called if you needed me."

"I know, and I appreciate you being there."

It never failed to amaze him how one tender look and a thank you could affect him. Living up to Miranda's expectations always made him prouder than even defending his country. "That's what husbands do."

"And I love you for being such a good one."

He leaned over and pressed a kiss to the top of her head, unable to resist the desire to touch her, to indulge himself in the simple pleasure of being together, to feel her hair against his mouth and inhale that lightly floral fragrance that haunted his fantasies when they were apart.

"So where do you want to start?" He knew she needed to take the lead, to trust he'd be by her side no matter what.

"If my grandfather was a BEL who worked in occupied France," she said, pulling up the hotel's Internet access, "then we have evidence to support the authenticity of the first marriage license."

"You sound like a lawyer."

"I happened to have studied pre-law. And let's not forget that both my parents are lawyers."

"The senator could have met your grandmother in France while he was stationed there."

She nodded. "My grandmother is the key here, Troy. We need to know more about her."

"Agreed. But Victoria and Laura hit a dead end with Laura Russell. We need to know about Laure Roussell."

Troy frowned at the computer monitor. "Yes, but without Victoria, how can we access the databases that'll give us this sort of information about a French citizen?"

She nodded absently, keying in an URL into the browser. "What about the genealogy sites? There's got to be information about the family online. That'll be a place to start."

"Good idea." Hiking a knee up onto the desk, he

swiveled around to watch her as she waited for a popular search engine to produce the results of some genealogy sites.

She bristled with intensity, an almost impatience as she manipulated her way through the Internet, quickly scanning and evaluating information before she decided the value of a site and moved on.

He loved her focus and intelligence. She'd always intended to go to law school, but had postponed her plans to marry him. And now that Troy thought about it, he hadn't heard her mention anything about resuming her studies in a long time.

Something about that bothered him, and he wasn't sure what. He knew logistics had been partially at fault for the delay. She'd wanted to wait until they'd gotten settled after the wedding before committing to the amount of energy law school would take. Then his orders had taken them from one coast to the other.

But they'd lived in Norfolk before their move to San Diego over a year ago, and he couldn't recall Miranda once mentioning feeling settled enough to tackle law school. Here was another reminder about how he hadn't been paying close enough attention to anything but his work.

And another clue he'd missed.

"I need more information." Miranda leaned back in her chair and glanced up at him. "Roussell isn't an uncommon name. I need to narrow my search, but I don't know anything about my grandmother. My mother just doesn't talk about her. I really don't think she remembers much. She was so young. Everything I know is just…*stuff*. Laura was the one compiling things her mother had said."

He motioned her to get up. "Let me on to my e-mail account. With any luck, your sister and Laura will have forwarded their information before your grandfather called this morning."

Troy suspected the posts would be there because he'd asked Laura to forward the information when he'd called her earlier. He'd also asked her to contact Adam and have him do the same. Troy logged on to his account, and sure enough, she'd accomplished another miracle. The posts were there. He made a mental note to remember that she and Dale got a decent wedding gift as thanks.

He quickly cut and paste the body of the e-mails into a Word document, so Miranda didn't notice the date and times of the posts, all of which had arrived *after* Victoria's visit.

"Looks like we've got some good stuff here," he said.

Leaning over his shoulder, Miranda peered at the screen, and he scrolled down the page taking in names, places, proposed dates that Laura had cataloged for their easy perusal.

One such item caught Miranda's attention.

"Look at this, Troy. I had no idea my grandmother painted, but Laura mentions it right there." She gave a laugh. "I suppose that explains Laura's mother and her interest."

"Makes me wonder why the senator would have opposed her career choice, doesn't it?" Troy scanned down the page to read the notes Adam had forwarded. "And look at this. Apparently Victoria knew. She wrote that your grandmother's portraits started all the trouble in the first place. The senator claims she wanted her work destroyed in the event of her death, and Laura's mother didn't believe him. Your mother never mentioned any of this to you?"

"I never asked," she said, and he thought he heard a hint of sadness in her voice. "Why would I bring up a painful subject just to satisfy my curiosity?"

But obviously Victoria had, and he cast her a sidelong glance, looking for some clue to her mood about her sister.

She just looked sad. And Troy wasn't surprised she'd reined in her own curiosity. That was Miranda—more caring and more generous to others than she was to herself. She looked out for the people she loved, which might explain why she was so select about who she cared for.

It was another realization about his wife that he'd missed, one he'd have to make a place for. She'd just mentioned her job as a sister. He had a responsibility as her husband to look out for her as much as she did for him.

"Wait a minute, Troy…" She trailed off with a look of comprehension dawning. Suddenly she slid into his lap and commandeered the keyboard. "Here, let me in."

Troy obliged, hiking her up higher to savor the full effects of her curvy bottom. She didn't seem to notice, so he pressed his advantage by looping his arms around her waist as she worked her way to a search engine to take another look.

"I saw a reference on one of these sites to a Roussell who was a painter." She maneuvered her way back through the history of the sites she'd visited. "Darn, I don't remember which one. It was just a mention, but it caught my eye."

"Run a fresh search," he suggested, taking the opportunity to massage the tense muscles in her shoulders and neck.

"Oh, that feels nice," she said before the Web kicked back enough hits to make her groan.

She searched through site after site that combined their keywords in any manner and even ran across several Roussells advertising printing and painting businesses before finally finding what she was looking for—a news item from a regional publication about a painting by a local artist housed in a private collection.

"Here it is," Miranda said, and Troy paused in his ministrations long enough to read the small piece, amazed she'd even noticed it. "Jean-Luc Roussell was a local artist from a village in the south of France, a farmer who'd gained renown for his landscapes in the early part of the last century."

"What's so interesting about him?" Troy left Miranda to scan the article as he began work again on her shoulders.

"This article is about one of his pieces being donated to a local museum. Oh, I see what's interesting." She sat upright as the piece caught her attention. "This is the only known painting of Jean-Luc Roussell's left in existence."

"What happened to the rest of them?"

"I'm not sure—no, here it is." Scrolling down on the screen, she scanned the plain unformatted text of the old article. "Apparently Jean-Luc Roussell was a war hero for refusing to let enemy soldiers commandeer his farm for their headquarters. They burned his art studio to the ground, murdered him then used his farm as their headquarters anyway. From what it says here, the enemy soldiers were ordered to destroy any of Roussell's work they came across as they ransacked the area to set an example."

"How did this painting survive?"

"Roussell gave it to his housekeeper as a birthday gift before the war began. She hid it, and after her death, her family donated it to their museum as part of local history." She sighed as she enlarged the image on the monitor. "Look at this piece. How sad that his art was destroyed."

Troy held no illusions about war. He believed in diplomacy above all else, but until that mentality translated globally, until differing principles and intolerance yielded to compromise and understanding, and above all *respect,* there would be a need for men like him to fight and defend their country.

"At least there's one left."

Often that was as good as it got. How many wars had destroyed entire cultures until all that remained was a memory that evolved into legend as generations passed?

"Such a shame—" Suddenly she sat bolt upright, almost colliding her head with his. "I don't believe this."

"What?"

"Look at the signature, Troy."

Peering over her shoulder, he glanced at the signature in the corner of the piece, which would have been indecipherable had she not enlarged the browser's view. The colorful landscape had been distorted by the enlargement, breaking into blurry pixels of bright colors, but the signature had swelled enough to make out the initials J.L.R. slashed in bold strokes over a symbol of a faint silver lion's head.

"I see it. What's so significant?"

Leaning back, she glanced up at him, and he couldn't miss the surprise in her eyes. "You see that lion's head?"

He nodded.

"It's the one imprinted on the head of my grandfather's cane."

14

MIRANDA LED TROY through the halls of Westfalls Academy, assailed by a past she hadn't thought of in forever. She'd reigned like a queen here once upon a time, but the halls now seemed smaller somehow, a casualty of perspective and age.

Troy gave a low whistle. "Highbrow place."

"True enough." She led him past the administrative offices where Laura's mother had worked through their school years.

The job had allowed Suzanne Granger to pay for her daughter's education and to be an active presence to ensure Laura was treated fairly and with respect. While her presence had accomplished that goal with the faculty, to Miranda's knowledge, it hadn't done a thing to facilitate Laura's acceptance among the student body.

Laura Granger, known among the student body as the strange ranger, had always been the odd one out. She'd had her circle of friends through the years, a group who hadn't fit into the mainstream any better than she did.

But now Miranda felt a lot more understanding about what it must have been like growing up so out of the loop. The school of life had taught her empathy. And what was really important.

Slipping her hand in Troy's, she walked along at his side, grateful for the lesson.

"Do you think your old art teacher will be able to help us?" he asked.

"If anyone can tell us what that symbol stands for, Mrs. Wellesley can. She's been on the faculty here forever. Although, I'm sure she wouldn't appreciate me phrasing it that way, or you calling her an 'old' art teacher, either."

Troy smiled. "I'm enjoying this blast from the past. Why haven't you ever brought me here before?"

"Westfalls was a long time ago." And she was glad to keep it there.

She wasn't especially proud of herself when she remembered her behavior toward Laura. While Miranda had never participated in any sort of physical action against her, she now knew how much being left out could hurt, and she cringed when recalling her intolerance and unkindness, the way she'd always excluded Laura.

And not because of dislike, either. Laura was right in this regard. They hadn't known each other at all. If by some miracle this family managed to moved past its problems, Miranda would put forth an effort to formulate another opinion of Laura—this time her own.

Steering Troy toward a staircase, Miranda said, "The art department is upstairs."

They found Mrs. Wellesley in her office. With her round cheeks and sunny smile, she looked as if she'd been sitting here ever since Miranda had left all those years ago. Older, perhaps, but just as familiar. And her office was *a lot* more cluttered with students' artwork from a staggering variety of media.

Miranda would bet that some of her own work—especially the ceramic tile that she'd painted as a Christmas gift for her favorite art teacher—was still tucked away somewhere on those shelves.

Mrs. Wellesley rose from behind her desk. "Miranda Ford, what a pleasure after all these years."

Miranda gave her a hug then introduced Troy, feeling a tingle of pride when she showed off her handsome husband.

It was a feeling she remembered from long ago, one she hadn't felt for a while. Not because she wasn't proud of the man she'd married, but because the feeling had the ability to make her feel out of balance, pressured, as if he didn't have as much to be proud of in her.

She'd missed this feeling, the almost giddy sense of excitement when she looked at him, so wildly gorgeous, so devoted and loving.

It was a feeling she wouldn't give away so lightly again.

Holding her head high, she said, "Troy and I are in town—"

"I know all about why you're here." She laughed. "I've been keeping up with your sister's columns. You're the featured honeymoon couple. Sounds like you've been having fun."

Troy flashed her one of his charming smiles. "A once in a lifetime experience."

They chatted for a few minutes, filling in the blanks on a lot of years. Unsurprisingly, Mrs. Wellesley knew much about Miranda. Around here, anyone who read the local paper could usually find some mention of the names Prescott and Ford.

"So what is it you wanted me to take a look at, dear?"

she asked, and Miranda removed from her purse a printed copy of the Jean-Luc Roussell's painting she'd tossed into an envelope. She explained they were interested in identifying the mark beneath the signature and understanding what it meant.

Mrs. Wellesley, true to form, didn't require any additional clarification and just fitted on the reading glasses dangling from a chain around her neck, pulled a magnifying glass from her desk drawer and took a closer look.

"Why, that's this artist's signature, dear."

"And the symbol?"

"Also part of his signature. Many artists simply sign their work, but some create their own mark, a device of self-expression, as it were. This one appears heraldic in design. See the way he uses only his initials transposed over this device? The lion certainly fits."

So why would her grandfather be walking around with a cane for more decades than she'd been alive with a familial device belonging to the Roussell family?

She hadn't been mistaken about her grandmother's name change, and Troy shot her a look that told her his thoughts headed down a similar path.

Mrs. Wellesley squinted down at the image. "Such a pity to have lost track of such a talent."

"We were surprised by that ourselves, Mrs. Wellesley," Troy admitted. "We couldn't find anything on this artist."

She nodded sadly. "If all his art was destroyed, then there would be no reason to register him. He wouldn't even have an entry in the Directories of Neglected Artists."

"Who are they?"

"Very obscure artists that only offbeat collectors and art sleuths are interested in."

Miranda stared down at the copied image of the sole remaining painting that she could only assume was of a landscape from somewhere around the artist's home. Art was not her area of expertise, but the colors were so vibrant, a neat trick of light and technique she assumed, because the whole look was somehow soft-edged and pretty. "It is a pity. This is such a magnificent painting. And I don't know why, but it's somehow familiar."

Mrs. Wellesley chuckled. "You don't know why it looks familiar?"

"No, should I?"

She gazed over the rim of her glasses and nodded. "Care to take a walk? I could do with getting out of this office, and I have a few minutes before my next class."

"Certainly." Troy took the lead, and moving to the door, he held it wide while Miranda followed Mrs. Wellesley from the office.

To Miranda's surprise, she led them outside and across the campus, where she inhaled deeply and held her face up to the bright late-afternoon sun.

"What a glorious day," she exclaimed. "I need to make it a point to get outside more often when the weather permits."

"After being in San Diego, I think Miranda must have forgotten what a real winter feels like," Troy said pleasantly as they crossed the summer lush quad and Miranda realized that Mrs. Wellesley was leading them back to her old dorm.

Marceaux House had been the newest building on

campus up until the recent addition of a performing arts center the alumni had financed a few years back. The dorm house had been erected with an endowment from the late Mireille Marceaux, who'd bequeathed Westfalls Academy her estate that, to Miranda's knowledge, *still* generated income.

As they stepped inside the grand foyer, Miranda remembered the pride she'd once felt to be a part of this house. Prestigious houses like Bradstreet and Stanton had long held impressive status because of the women they commemorated, but they paled in light of the secrecy surrounding the endowment from the mysterious artist.

She also remembered how unhappy she'd been that Laura had been a part of that glory, too. They'd been in the same year and it had been enough to share classes and activities, but sharing Marceaux House had always felt like a nasty joke.

But perhaps it had only been a missed opportunity.

They entered the foyer, a formal reception area where the housemistress could greet guests. A huge stone fireplace dominated the room, which Miranda knew was kept lit throughout the winter with the mantel decorations changed to reflect the various holidays. There was a mudroom tucked discreetly to the side, and she knew from personal experience that there'd be hell to pay for any student who tracked snow over the pristine floor.

She'd been a quick study though, and had only been forced to scrub the foyer's massive wooden floor once before she made a trip into that mudroom every time she walked in the door.

Above the fireplace, in a display case that looked remarkably like the one in Laura's Wedding Wing, was the first and grandest of the dozen Mireille Marceaux landscapes adorning the walls of Marceaux House.

The painting was titled *Dawn Splendor* and depicted a scene of a sunrise breaking over a ridge in violent shades of lavender and crimson, not unlike the ridge where Troy had taken her to hike and fish. Mireille Marceaux had a gift for painting the nuances of nature, and the striking colors combined with the dramatic use of light and shadow created a scene that seemed glorious, almost living.

"Do you see it now?" Mrs. Wellesley asked never taking her gaze from the painting with an almost loving expression.

"You're right," Troy said. "I don't know a thing about art, but I can see similarities. The way it all comes together, the colors…I don't know."

"The composition, dear." She turned to Miranda. "Don't you agree?"

After living in this house and looking at Mireille Marceaux's art for nine years… "It's incredible. I can't believe I didn't recognize the similarities sooner."

"The styles are the closest I've seen, as a matter of fact." Mrs. Wellesley smiled. "Who knows? Maybe our local legend and this unknown French painter studied beneath the same master. They're both French and lived during the middle of the last century. It's possible."

She and Troy exchanged glances, and Miranda could tell that he was as surprised as she. A connection between these two artists hadn't even been a consideration.

Miranda glanced down at her copy of Roussell's painting, at the unusual signature. She stared at that symbol, the way the monogram had been artistically crafted over that familiar device…and then comprehension dawned.

"Mireille Marceaux never signed her work, either," she whispered more to herself than to her companions.

Then another similarity hit her.

"Ohmigosh! How on earth did I miss this? M. M. Melts in your mouth not—"

She stopped before blurting out the rest of the slogan that students in her years had used to joke about the Mireille Marceaux erotic paintings hidden somewhere on the campus. Horrified, she turned to stare at Mrs. Wellesley, who stared back with a raised brow.

"Forgive me," she said. "I was remembering an old saying from my school days."

"I'm well aware of the saying, dear."

Miranda remembered *that* tone from long ago, too.

"You think Mireille Marceaux and this artist used initials to sign their work because they had the same teacher, too?" Troy stepped in with the question to give her a chance to recover.

Her hero.

Mrs. Wellesley nodded. "It's certainly plausible." She chuckled. "All these years of mystery surrounding our local legend and you might have added another piece to the puzzle. But you couldn't find anything about this artist?"

Troy moved closer, slipping his arm around Miranda's waist, a perfectly timed move as her knees were turning to jelly.

"No, I'm afraid," Miranda said, not sure at all what to make of this connection and not wanting to reveal any more information until she was.

Mrs. Wellesley fell silent and stared at the copy of the painting that raised so many questions. "Have you tried the museum directories?"

"I'm not familiar with them," Miranda replied. And she wasn't sure she wanted to be. Not when her head was spinning with all the implications of this conversation.

"Your artist could have a biographical entry in the system. Even with one piece on display. It all depends on the size and nature of the museum."

"Can we access this directory on the Internet?" Troy asked.

She shrugged. "I'm not sure if you can, but I have access through one of my art organizations. If you'd like, you're welcome to take a look under my access information. You can use my office while I'm in my class."

Miranda reached out to take the older woman's hands. "Thank you. You've been so helpful."

"The pleasure's mine, dear. I love seeing my students keeping up their interest in art."

She might not be so pleased if she knew Miranda's interest had nothing to do with the art and everything to do with the artists. Miranda couldn't even process that thought yet, and by the way Troy was hanging on to her as they walked back across the campus, he knew it, too.

Fortunately Mrs. Wellesley's students began gathering soon after they returned to her office so they were spared from sharing any more surprises when she logged on to her account, gave Miranda a hug, then headed off to class.

Troy didn't say a word as he leaned over her and she searched through database after database looking for the French museum that housed Jean-Luc Roussell's only existing painting.

Nothing.

Apparently the museum displaying his piece was an institution with only works of local interest and didn't participate in any loan programs with their collections.

"Get out of here and on to the Internet," Troy said.

"Why?"

"I want to check for information about the town. Most towns have area attraction guides. Maybe there'll be something there. It's the only place we haven't tried yet."

"Good idea."

Miranda keyed in the name of the town into a search engine and pulled up the town's official Web site. Sure enough there was a link to the museum, and her heart began to race as she navigated her way through the site structure to the work on display. Her hands shook when she keyed in her artist's name. She hit the enter key…

Two short paragraphs appeared. The first a description of the painting; the second a biography of the artist.

Troy's grip tightened on her shoulder as they read the brief synopsis of the artist's life. There was summary of his death and the destruction of his art almost identical to the one reported in the news article, and there was mention of his only surviving family. One sentence that turned out to contain all the information they needed.

Jean-Luc Roussell had one daughter, another talented painter who'd studied under him. This young woman joined the French Resistance to avenge her father's death and never returned to her home after the war.

There it was, the connection she needed live on the Internet for the whole world to view. *If* anyone knew enough to look. She suspected none did.

Except for one man.

Miranda guessed why Laure Roussell had never returned to her hometown…because she'd met up with William Marshall Prescott, married him, changed her name to Laura and relocated to the United States.

THIS UNEXPECTED TURN of events provided Troy with another chance to drive home how he intended to stand beside Miranda for better or worse. Unfortunately, he agreed with her opinion that this situation didn't qualify as *better*.

"You couldn't have foreseen this, Miranda." He steered the car down the tree-lined driveway leading away from Westfalls Academy.

"No, I couldn't have, which was precisely my argument in the first place. Grandfather had a reason for keeping his secrets. No question. And I walked right into it. This isn't happening." She exhaled a sigh of utter desperation and lowered her face into her hands.

Had he not known she was genuinely upset, he might have enjoyed this rare moment of melodrama. Miranda rarely, if ever, let her emotions get the better of her.

Except in bed. There, she became putty in his hands.

"*We* walked right into it," he corrected. "The senator could have asked you to stop searching and trust him that any secrets were best left in the past."

Miranda groaned and he shifted his gaze off the road long enough to catch her shudder. "He didn't need to. *I* said that the instant Victoria and Laura told us their plan. Just because he lied didn't change that, or give us carte blanche to start digging up the past."

Troy couldn't argue. "But should haves or could haves can't help us now. We're in the middle of a situation we didn't expect and need to figure out what to do about it."

"Should I say anything to Mrs. Wellesley, do you think? Ask her not to mention that we'd come by?"

"Who's she going to mention it to?" He frowned. "Miranda, you can't ask her not to be curious, and if you try to cover your tracks you'll only make her wonder why you want her to. Leave it alone. She doesn't have a clue why you were interested in an artist with the initials J.L.R. Even if she pursues the connection to your local legend, she has no way to connect him to your family."

Miranda finally glanced up, and her stricken expression eased somewhat. "I know you're right."

"But it's not making you feel any better?"

She gave a dry laugh. "I'm sailing in uncharted waters, that's all. Snooping is Victoria's department. She can obviously handle the stress."

He suspected his sister-in-law thought the stress was an adrenaline rush. "I wouldn't stress too much because we can't confirm any of this. From what you've told me, people have been speculating about your local legend for years. The only choice you have to make now is whether to forget what we've learned or go to the senator and *negotiate* some sort of truce. Victoria and Laura have set their weddings up as a place where your mothers can hook up again. Your job is figuring out how to get the senator not to take away that chance."

"You know, Troy, I'm not sure that we can't confirm all this ourselves. You told me the BELs were sent in to mobilize the rebel forces. From what I remember about the French Resistance, they were infamous for hit-and-run attacks that thwarted the enemy.

"And Victoria mentioned my grandfather and some sort of transportation bombing. I wouldn't have remembered."

Troy nodded. "So what do you want to do?"

"As much as I don't want to, I need to see my grandfather. *Before* Victoria's column comes out. Things need to be out on the table and he needs to know that all we want is a chance for our mothers to make peace. Without his blessing, I think Laura's right—this won't happen." She shook her head and let her eyes flutter shut. "And here I was afraid Victoria would be the one to give him a heart attack. You were right, too, Troy, this is blackmail."

"It's *negotiation*." He turned the car in the direction of the family mansion, and hoped like hell he was right.

15

MIRANDA WAITED UNTIL Troy opened her car door, taking the opportunity to steel her nerves. To her surprise, it wasn't facing her grandfather that troubled her. It was facing him *alone*. And she would have to, no matter how much she wanted Troy with her. Respect demanded that she not air this situation in front of anyone—not even her husband. Not if she wanted any hope of getting her grandfather to cooperate.

Her chances were slim enough already.

But she'd promised to play things straight with Troy and had been taking steps to open up. It struck her how much she wanted to continue doing that, how much she wanted him by her side as she faced what was sure to be a difficult confrontation. But proximity didn't necessarily mean togetherness. Sharing feelings did. She just now understood the difference.

And how the very same reasoning might apply when Troy was deployed, too.

When Troy appeared at her side of the car, she smiled up at him and said, "I hate to ask this, Troy, but—"

"You need to talk with the senator alone."

"Would you mind terribly?"

"I know the drill. I'll go run interference with your parents and buy you all the time you need. Sound good?"

Rising to her feet, she swayed forward, coming flush up against him. "I love you, Lieutenant Commander."

Never one to miss an opportunity, Troy fastened his arms around her, pulling her close. "And I love you, Mrs. Knight."

Feeling the familiarity of his body against hers was exactly what she needed most right now, and she vowed that she wasn't ever going to rely on proximity again to feel close to her husband. Not ever again. "Lucky me."

Dropping a kiss onto the top of her head, he steered her toward the stairs. "Don't take any guff. I won't be far if you need me."

"I know." And she did. He'd be there to support her no matter what. She only had to let him.

As sure as she was of Troy's support, she was equally unsure of her grandfather's response, so she anchored her mood with her husband's love to get her through the meeting ahead.

Using her key, she let them into the house, pausing inside the entryway. "It's not time for dinner, so I'm guessing Grandfather will be in his study. I don't have a clue where my parents are."

"I'll find them. But don't take too long." He flashed her a grin that made his green eyes sparkle. "I've still got a prize to claim."

"I won't forget."

She couldn't possibly. One decision and lots of sex toys had made a difference. No more running and hiding. She would face what was ahead, *whatever* that might be.

After kissing his cheek, she hurried down the hallway toward her grandfather's study, rapped on the door and stepped inside when he invited her in.

He stood at the window again, leaning heavily on his cane, and she wondered if his leg bothered him today, an occurrence affected by both weather and activity. When he glanced at her, he didn't look surprised, just met her gaze with a grave expression of his own.

"I wondered if you'd be back," he said.

"You did?"

He nodded, his dark gaze inscrutable. "I know you, Miranda. You're intelligent and determined. You understand what's going on with people, the things they don't always say. You're a lot like me, if you don't mind me saying. But even so, I couldn't grasp how you might handle this situation."

She only nodded, not minding the comparison. So many people called him grim and severe, and while he was definitely those things, he had many other qualities to balance them out, qualities she'd come to hold in high regard as he'd generously shared them through her lifetime.

"I've placed you in a difficult position," he said. "Your sister, too. I've forced you to make decisions when I couldn't anticipate what choices you'd make."

Did that mean he cared what choices they made? She wanted to ask why he was prepared to alienate even more family members by backing them all into corners, but diplomacy and restraint won out. "You're asking Victoria to give up her family."

"No, I'm asking her to not dig up a past that has no place in the future."

"She just wants to understand."

"That's your sister." To her surprise, she heard no censure in his voice, and if she didn't know better, she'd have thought he sounded approving. "Curious and fascinated by everyone and everything around her. She's a lot like your grandmother was, along with headstrong, committed to her causes and so loving she's always a joy to be around."

Miranda exhaled a breath she hadn't been aware of holding. That he'd actually brought up her grandmother seemed surprising alone, but that his opinion of Victoria sounded nothing like a criticism came as an even greater surprise.

She wasn't sure how to reply. His words belied his expression. His dark eyes revealed so much she didn't understand, and she could only guess at his mood, pensive and defeated.

Yesterday he'd seemed old, but this…this was somehow so much more. This was as if the weight of eighty years had slammed him in his chest, cutting off air and making him wither around his edges.

"Grandfather, are you—"

"I placed my daughters in the same situation, Miranda."

The words fell heavily between them. A truth that even unspoken held power. She felt guilty for standing here, for making him face truths that were clearly a burden, and she would have spared him if she could, would have told him not to relive such a painful experience for her benefit.

But she couldn't. This was not about him. It had never been only about him. His decisions had affected his daughters' lives, had dripped like poison into the next generation.

This wasn't about her, either. Miranda had to stand her ground no matter how much it hurt. Her grandfather needed to talk because she needed to understand how to help him fix things. For Victoria. For their mother. And, yes, Miranda realized, for herself, too.

So she could look herself in the mirror and know she hadn't hidden from the problem. She'd tackled it head on and done her best. No matter what happened next.

"Please help me understand why, Grandfather. I don't understand why any of this is happening." Bracing her hands on the back of a wing chair, she suddenly felt too restless to sit, and too unsteady to stand without support.

But she sounded calm and resolute, and that was a start.

"My daughters were so young. I made their choices for them. But you and your sister are grown women. I can't choose for you. I guessed your sister would go full steam ahead with her plans and live with the consequences. But I wondered what you'd do."

"Victoria stopped searching."

He inclined his snowy white head, his eyes never leaving hers. "I know. She called me. But I promise that won't be the end of this. She won't back down. As we speak, she's figuring out some way to outmaneuver me."

He was right. He might have cut off the past for Victoria, but he hadn't taken away the future. She would respond in the morning's newspaper by announcing her double wedding with Laura Granger. She had outmaneuvered him, and not without cost. But Victoria was willing to pay that price because she had the courage to fight for what she wanted—her family back together.

While Miranda might not understand how her sister could marry a stranger, she did understand love. Love could help someone overcome her obstacles. Love could help someone grow.

Love had helped her find the courage to stop running and hiding.

"Victoria is respecting your wishes, Grandfather. She's stopped searching for answers about our grandmother. She'd rather make you happy than answer her questions."

"And you?"

That dark gaze bore into her, but Miranda met it evenly. "No, not me."

"What is the point of all this? I know you, Miranda. You don't act without a reason."

She'd said exactly the same thing about him and mentally formed the words before speaking them aloud, committing to them. "Victoria, Laura and *I* believe our mothers miss each other. We want to give them a chance to get together again if that's what they want. Whatever took place in the past shouldn't keep apart people who love each other."

After a deep breath to steel her resolve, Miranda explained about Tyler Tripp's video and the events that had fueled her epiphanies this week.

"Watching Victoria with Laura made me realize how far she and I have grown apart, and not just us, but this entire family. Grandfather, I've never had any use for Laura, that's no secret, but when I opened my eyes and took a closer look, I saw she's not so different from Victoria and me. This grand opening has forced us to look at each other with fresh eyes and a better understanding of how our family situation has impacted us."

How one man's expectations had affected his family.

"I think Mother deserves a chance to make peace with her sister if that's what she wants. I'll handle dealing with the Grangers to make her happy. Who knows, if I keep an open mind about them I might even be surprised."

His gaze never wavered, and for the life of her, Miranda couldn't get a read on his reaction. Nothing but a silence that fell so heavy she couldn't even hear their breathing.

They'd reached stalemate. He wasn't going to make this easy, wasn't going to pick up where she'd left off and offer a solution. She'd originally come to him for that purpose, for guidance on how to deal with the past.

He hadn't given it to her. He'd lied instead. And now she had to ask if he'd been running from ugly emotions, too, hiding from his own painful truths.

She suspected the answer, and understood.

"Will you let us give Mother the chance to get together with her sister or will you force her to choose between you and Victoria?"

His grip tightened on the cane as if he was bracing himself. "I'll lose her if I force her to choose."

The conviction in his voice belied his expression, a drawn, overwhelmed look that suddenly frightened her. If he already knew he'd lose, then why had he called Victoria?

"Can't we leave the past in the past?" she asked. "What is so horrible about this family being together? Please tell me so I can understand, so I can help."

And to Miranda's horror, his stoic demeanor, that familiar, strong presence seemed to crumble before her very eyes. Suddenly he just looked old, and defeated.

She quickly went to him. "Please come sit."

He allowed her to assist him to the chair behind his desk, which drove home how right she was to worry. Kneeling before him, she asked, "Shall I call Rutger?"

He shook his head. "Not if you want your explanation."

"Are you up to it?"

His expression softened, not a smile, *never* a smile, but some hint of irony that suggested if he'd been up to explaining, he would have long ago.

She touched the cane he still held, thumbed the silver headpiece, the symbol she'd seen her whole life that had taken on such unexpected meaning. "Does it have to do with this?"

"How much did you find out?"

"Only that this symbol is the one a French artist used as a signature on a painting. An artist named Jean-Luc Roussell."

The little color he had drained away, leaving Miranda with the wild thought that she would be responsible for giving him that heart attack.

Propping the cane against the desk, she reached out to take his unsteady hands, to reassure him, "I haven't said anything to anyone, Grandfather. Except for Troy. He's been helping me make sense of the whole situation."

"So you know."

"Only enough to guess at the rest…Was Jean-Luc Roussell my great-grandfather?"

He nodded.

"So it's true. Laure Roussell was Mireille Marceaux."

Every fiber of her being wanted to understand how a woman who'd fought for the French Resistance and married an American politician had wound up living a secret double life as an erotic artist, but when he didn't reply, she went to the bar to pour him a glass of water.

Her grandfather looked so frail that she thought her heart would break, and she hated being responsible for adding to his grief. For one terrible moment, she wished she'd kept her mouth shut and hadn't brought the past crashing down on all their heads.

But logically Miranda knew this was only a knee-jerk reaction to an emotionally difficult situation. A habit she'd developed from a lot of years spent avoiding conflicts.

Retreat had seemed so much easier. And in some ways it had been. But the simple fact was that one could only assume so much responsibility. This situation went a lot further back than she did. And if she had to replay the course of events that led her to this study, she would make the same choices again.

She'd learned from the experience.

Playing life safe wasn't the only way to play, wasn't always the *best* way. Victoria had taught her that. Some things were worth fighting for, worth dealing with the consequences.

Bringing her family together was one of those things.

She placed the water glass on his desk, but her grandfather ignored it, reached for his cane and pushed heavily to his feet. Moving back to the window, he stared outside.

"Laure Roussell was your grandmother," he said quietly. "And she was a magnificent woman..."

He told her the story of how he'd met a courageous young Resistance fighter when he'd been dropped behind enemy lines in occupied France. A select group of officers had been specially trained to mobilize the rebel forces in preparation for the Normandy Invasion, and he'd been assigned to make contact with a woman named Laure Roussell, who commanded a large faction in a strategically critical region.

He'd made that contact, and had gone underground with the Resistance. For nearly a year, he and Laure had fought together under extreme conditions, sabotaging the enemy's lines of transportation to cut off their supplies and arms.

Until the enemy caught up with them.

Miranda already knew the story about how her grandfather had been imprisoned in a concentration camp, long months spent as a prisoner of war, enduring physical torture while he watched his men brutalized and executed. She knew his leg injury had been a result, a wound he'd carried all his adult life to make sure he never forgot.

But she hadn't known the men in that camp hadn't been his, or that their torture had been the enemy's efforts to locate and crush her grandmother's rebel forces.

Neither he nor any of the rebels had betrayed anything at all about Commander Roussell. They were loyal to her and the cause, and Miranda's grandfather had loved her.

"She continued the work after our imprisonment," he said, his voice distant, emotion carefully concealed behind a veil of years. "She received my orders and led her people in a critical raid so our forces could infiltrate. She carried out my mission objective. Our government honored her with a medal."

Miranda hadn't known that, either.

"We'd been married in a small church in her hometown before my capture. After my escape from the concentration camp, I was smuggled into England for rehabilitation. When the war was over, she joined me."

Miranda tried to make sense of these events, already

knew something must have gone tragically wrong, or else how had her grandmother traveled from Laure Roussell, French Resistance fighter to Laura Russell, political wife and loving mother, to Mireille Marceaux, renowned painter?

These were logic leaps she couldn't make, and she waited for the explanation, waited while her grandfather stared out the window as if he could see back to a time and place where he'd allowed himself to live and feel.

And hurt.

When it became evident that he'd gotten lost in his memories, she asked, "If she was honored for her service to our country, why did she change her name?"

"Because I asked her to," he said simply. "She loved me enough to sacrifice who she was to become who I needed her to be—the perfect wife and mother." He held up the cane. "She gave me this. She placed her heritage in my hands and trusted me to care for it."

The sight of his fierce grip on the Roussell family device made Miranda ache in a way she'd never ached before. She still didn't understand, but she knew he felt he hadn't lived up to her trust, that he'd failed the woman he loved and had been bearing the weight of that failure for too long.

"She campaigned by my side, involved herself in all the right causes to further my political career and reflect well on our family. Even my parents and grandparents were impressed with her, and they weren't easily impressed. I barely lived up to their expectations."

Miranda found it hard to imagine her grandfather not meeting anyone's expectations. He exemplified a principle-fighting overachiever way beyond anyone she'd ever known, but as she had only vague recollections of her great-grandparents, she could only guess at how high the family expectations had been. Too high, she guessed.

Far too high.

"She loved me and our girls enough to sacrifice herself to live the life I'd chosen for us. God, how she loved our girls."

He bowed his head and, even in profile, Miranda could see pain etch sharp grooves on his face, the way he closed his eyes and inhaled as if looking for strength. She was reminded of the young man he'd once been in the picture Victoria had shown her.

A man who hadn't smiled. Had he ever smiled?

She didn't know. The only thing she knew right now was that this family's expectations had claimed too much from all of them. The members of each generation had tried to meet those too-high expectations or had rebelled against them, but each generation had given up parts of their souls along the way.

Miranda understood what had compelled her grandmother to live life behind a mask. She'd obviously loved her husband and daughters enough to put aside the passionate woman she was, except for the secret moments when she allowed herself to live with her whole heart and soul. Like Victoria, she'd apparently understood that without living life to the fullest, the soul withered until one no longer had the ability to smile.

She wondered when her grandfather had last smiled.

Too long ago.

And she hadn't understood until this very second that she'd been striving to live up to those expectations, too, struggling and sacrificing to achieve a perfection that didn't exist because life wasn't perfect, *couldn't* be perfect.

Miranda watched her grandfather, her heart aching because he'd never allowed himself to simply be a man with strengths and flaws, a man who could laugh and cry, a man who could let himself be loved. She wanted to go to him, place her arms around him and give him a hug, so he knew he wasn't alone.

But one simply didn't hug her grandfather, and before she could decide what to do, he said, "She was the perfect wife and mother. The perfect daughter-in-law. The perfect hostess. And I was content with that. I never questioned what the cost would be. My passionate, strong wife suddenly contained in the box of the life I was comfortable leading."

Another person who'd lost so much precious time because of this family's obsession with perfection.

"What happened?" she asked softly.

"She died."

He fell silent for so long that she wondered if he'd retreated so deep in self-reflection that he'd forgotten she was even here.

But then he straightened and when he spoke his voice was stronger, harder. "I received the call right here in this study. It was the last weekend of the month when Laure always traveled into the city for her monthly Women's Club meeting. She'd been on her way home. The girls had come home for a school break and my mother had been putting them to bed when the phone rang. The officer told me there'd been an accident. The driver in the other car had been drunk. He passed out, crossed the lane and hit her head-on. They both died instantly."

Miranda was struck by visions of her mother, all of six years old, being tucked into bed only to awaken in the morning to find that the mother she loved wouldn't be coming home.

Life's too short, big sis. Lighten up and enjoy yourself, Victoria had told her.

When had her sister gotten so wise?

"I'd just decided to wait until the morning to break the news to the girls when the second call came." The hardness in her grandfather's voice didn't hide the hollowness she heard there, and Miranda braced herself, not wanting to hear how such a tragedy could grow even worse, knowing she had to.

"Who called, Grandfather?"

"Laure's lawyer. He told me she'd retained him to deliver a letter to me in the event of her death, that he had to drive in from the city and would arrive shortly before dawn. He asked me not to announce her death until I'd read her letter."

Inhaling deeply, he tightened his grip on the cane, visibly steeling himself, and Miranda did the same, waiting, her sense of foreboding nearly overwhelming, despite her resolve.

"Her letter explained everything. The monthly Women's Club meetings she'd been attending for years had actually been visits to an art studio in New York City. While I thought she'd been dabbling in a hobby at home, content to paint portraits of our daughters, she'd been painting with a passion and taking her work into the city to show.

"For one weekend a month, she lived as she'd been born to. But I forced her into living a secret life that I never suspected. I'd blinded myself because I needed to believe she was content. And that one letter proved how wrong I'd been."

"You had no idea?" The question slipped out as a pained whisper when she realized what a shock learning about her grandmother's secret career must have been.

He shook his head. "She'd started as a lark. That weekend was her private getaway, a way to replenish her soul, but then her career exploded. She found solace in her work, an outlet for her passion, the *life* I forced her to keep inside."

Forced? Miranda heard the bitterness, wasn't sure she understood.

"She felt guilty." He gave a harsh laugh. "She knew I associated her painting with her life back in France, and I'd shut out anything about that time. In her letter, she explained that she'd tried to abandon her painting, but it was such a part of her…she feared I'd learn her secret and be hurt. Even though I forced her to hide who she was, she only cared about hurting me. She'd planned for every eventuality so she couldn't be connected to Mireille Marceaux. No publicity. No paper trail. The only people who knew her identity were her art dealer and lawyer.

"On that one weekend a month, she worked in the gallery as an assistant, mingling with people who celebrated her art. But no one knew who she was. She even planned for death to make sure the money she'd earned would be dispersed so there would never be a need for the media or lawyers or anyone to start following her finances. She dotted every I and crossed every T."

Westfalls Academy suddenly made sense. She'd left her fortune to her daughters' school. "Oh, Grandfather."

"I was so angry." He closed his eyes and bowed his head. "I had to be. If I wasn't I'd have had to face that my need to forget the war had driven the woman I loved into hiding. I brought her to this country because I couldn't live without her. But I abandoned her here. I needed to forget the war so much that I tried to erase every memory. Even in her. I molded her into the perfect society wife and nearly killed her soul and her passion—the very things I fell in love with.

"I was angry because if I wasn't, I'd have had to face that I would rather sacrifice the woman I loved than slay my own dragons. I was responsible for driving her away and robbing my daughters of the mother who loved them so much. All because I couldn't face the memories of what happened inside that concentration camp. To our men. To me…"

Miranda didn't know when she'd started to cry, but silent tears welled in her throat, a lump of emotion that choked her.

"Laure tried for years to convince me to get help, but I was too proud. If I hid how hard I was struggling, the problem would go away. But she loved me enough to be who I needed her to be. Except for that one weekend a month."

He finally met her gaze, and she could see the weight of the truth in his eyes, the sorrow. "She was a magnificent woman, Miranda. Instead of hiding from all the tragedy of the war, she'd faced it and learned a precious life lesson—to love as if every moment was her last. So she loved me that way, and our girls. It has taken me decades to face this, to understand that to be the mother our girls deserved, she couldn't let her soul die. Even if she had to hide. In order to love us, she couldn't let anyone take away who she was, not even me…."

His words trailed off, fading to a hollow quiet that punctuated the truth, and the distance between them. Tears slipped down Miranda's cheeks, and she stood there, watching him, her own heart breaking, the silence so complete.

She ached for this strong man, who'd borne the crushing weight of this truth all alone. Instead of embracing his family and comforting each other in grief, he'd pushed everyone away. He'd been so devastated that he hadn't even allowed his daughters to take comfort in each other. He'd hidden his heartache the same way her grandmother had hidden her painting.

And Miranda ached for two little girls who'd gone to bed one night never suspecting how tragically their lives would change when they awoke, never taking comfort in knowing how much their mother had loved them.

How much their father still did.

"Mother should know." Her words were a whisper that would bridge the distance between them, *if* he would let her.

He inclined his head, and when he finally turned to face her, there were tears in his eyes, too. "I know."

She willed him to understand that only he could choose to face the past and let his family back into his life, to accept their love and support and stop hiding.

To love as if each day was the last.

She could take the first step, but he had to let himself be included.

And Miranda understood that this was a lesson she needed to learn, too.

Life was growing and learning and achieving and, yes, failing, too. Life was ups and downs and handling them with the people she loved. She had no right to deny herself and Troy the pleasures and experiences of being a man and woman who loved each other.

Because that's what they were—people with strengths and weaknesses, who could live and love and grow together.

If only she let them.

So she went to her grandfather. She placed her hand over his where he held the Roussell family device so tightly within his grasp, and raised up to kiss his cheek.

"I love you, Grandfather."

And when he opened his arms to her, Miranda knew she'd done the right thing.

16

TROY HAD EXPECTED opposition when he insisted on parading Miranda blindfolded through the Wedding Wing, but to her credit, she made the trip in stride. He kept a firm hold on her arm and led her from their suite to the elevator then down to the lobby.

They'd gotten a few smiles from the desk clerks, but he didn't mention them. After the night she'd had wondering about what was happening with her mother and grandfather, he led her past *The Falling Woman,* bypassing another reminder of the long-hidden truths that were currently being revealed between people she cared about.

It wasn't until he'd steered her inside the spa then followed an attendant into a special room that he finally brought her to a halt and untied the blindfold.

"Okay, Mrs. Knight. Open your eyes."

Miranda took one look around the tiled room, where a small oval pool bubbled with fragrant brown mud and an entire wall comprised an open shower, and frowned at him.

"I thought you rolled around in enough mud on land maneuvers, Lieutenant Commander."

"I do. But I have a prize to collect and I want to collect it here."

"In the mudroom?"

"Rolling around in the mud will make *you* happy."

"Troy, we don't have to do this just because I want to. I won't mind—"

"Yes, we do." There was no room for argument here. "You put a smile on your face when I took you fishing. Consideration works both ways."

"Fishing wasn't so bad."

"I don't care if mud bathing is worse than furniture shopping. I'll wallow in it to make you happy. Fair's fair."

She gazed up at him with a searching expression then inclined her head. "Okay."

"No debate?"

He'd expected one. It had taken him too long to identify that Miranda wasn't nearly as comfortable *being* accommodated as she was *accommodating,* but now that he'd finally opened his eyes, he intended to repay her consideration in kind.

"What's there to debate? You're right. Fair's fair. And if you really want to collect your prize here… I'm an accommodating wife."

Now it was his turn to eye her curiously, but she just smiled invitingly and started unbuttoning his shirt.

"This won't be nearly as painful as furniture shopping," she said.

"That's a promise?"

"It is." Her blue eyes sparkled as she tugged the shirt from his waistband. "We'll sit in that cool mud and relax—"

"And you'll tell me what your mother said when she called this morning."

"And I'll tell you what my mother said when she

called this morning." Miranda's smile widened as she dragged his sleeves down his arms.

Troy waited as she hung his shirt on a hook then returned for his pants. His blood began to hum, every nerve on edge because he'd been anticipating his prize. Her smile struck him as mysterious, enticing, an invitation to great sex.

And then there was the way she touched him... She had that familiar determination she used to get after he'd been away too long. Ready. Hungry. Wanting to take the lead and ensure he satisfied her the way she wanted to be satisfied.

This was one of his favorite things about marriage to Miranda—watching the bold, sensual woman emerge when she let her hair down.

He wanted her to let that mane of silky curls fall down her back and keep it there.

"Mother called to tell me she was going to a storage facility to arrange to have Grandmother's paintings brought home today." She dragged his pants down.

"So Laura's mother was right. Your grandmother hadn't wanted the paintings destroyed."

Miranda shook her head, making him struggle to concentrate when she unleashed a promising erection, her smooth fingers making his body come to life in her hands.

"Actually, no," she said. "My grandmother did leave instructions for her paintings to be destroyed. She didn't want anything left behind to connect her art to Mireille Marceaux's. She knew people might notice the similarities like Mrs. Wellesley did." She gazed up at him with a soft expression. "Grandfather couldn't bring himself to destroy them. Not when they were all his daughters would ever have of her."

"So Victoria was right," he said thoughtfully. "The senator was devastated when she died."

Troy could understand. After Miranda had delivered her mother to her grandfather's study last night, she'd given him the synopsized version of the senator's revelations on the ride to the hotel. They'd decided to sit back and wait while the senator worked things out with his daughters.

And so far, so good.

Even the publication of Victoria's column in this morning's paper seemed anticlimactic by comparison. Except to the town. It wasn't yet noon, and Adam had told them that the morning edition had already sold out of the stands and a local television network wanted to send a crew for the wedding, turning this denouement into a live media circus.

Also according to Adam, the brides were pleased the story would be picked up on the local network. Not only could this sort of coverage spread the magic of Falling Inn Bed, but a little family unity would go a long way toward putting the fascination with this family to rest once and for all. And since both camps remained silent about the weddings, it appeared that everyone stood united behind this event.

He hoped that turned out to be true.

His sister-in-law and Laura wanted family unity, and he suspected they were about to get a lot more than they'd bargained for. Neither of them had a clue yet about the forces mobilizing at the family mansion, or the enormity of the secrets to be revealed. The families would get to put their rusty togetherness skills to the test when they decided how best to deal with Laure Roussell's many identities.

"So what's going to happen with Laura's mom?"

"Mother says after she makes the arrangements to have the art shipped back to the house, she'll pay her sister a visit."

"Alone?"

"I offered to go, but she wants to do this herself."

"She'll be okay?"

Miranda nodded. "She sounded…good. Here's a chance to fix things, and you know Mother, she loves a good challenge."

"What about Victoria and Laura?"

"Laura's out of my jurisdiction, but Mother's leaning toward surprising Victoria at the wedding tomorrow. I told her go for it. Victoria has no idea who'll show up and who won't, so we'll show up together as a wedding gift. She likes surprises."

"I like that." He liked this side of his wife, too. She seemed at peace with the unfolding events, at ease in a way she hadn't been for too long.

Slipping his arms around her, he pulled her close, aligning all her curves with his. She exhaled a breathy sigh that made him smile, and he reached for the zipper at her nape, deciding it was time to see some skin.

"Should be some party. What about your grandfather? Think he'll come, too?"

She lifted her hair to help him access the zipper. "I suppose that depends on how this afternoon goes between mother and Aunt Suzanne."

Aunt Suzanne.

He couldn't imagine life without his family—even scattered around the globe as they were. Knowing he could pick up the phone any time effectively erased time zones. He wanted Miranda to have that kind of family support, too. People she felt close to. People she could share her life with. He sensed the future held lots of possibilities for this family, and he liked that Miranda had grabbed them with both hands.

Now if they could just overcome a few obstacles in their lives…

Troy might have to amend his goal of getting her to share what had been going on at home, but he wasn't too disappointed. They were moving in that direction. Many things had changed since their arrival at this hotel. Miranda had assumed control of the situation and was opening up to excellent results.

Her mood had also improved dramatically, and she hadn't put on her perfect smile and pretended everything was okay since her confrontation with Victoria. She'd been sharing her thoughts, and he intended to put forth the effort to help her continue this trend at home.

"Thanks for being so understanding with all the time we've had to spend dealing with my family on our vacation." Letting her dress slither to the floor, she snuggled against him, and the contact of all her curves shot his pulse into the red zone.

"My pleasure. I like when you appreciate me."

"I do, you know," she whispered against his lips, dragging her tongue against his mouth in a kiss that tasted like a promise. "You won our bet, and I can be a *very* gracious loser."

"That's what I like best about playing games with

you—it doesn't seem to matter who wins or loses. Now, I want you to get naked and in that mud."

"Is that a command?"

"It is."

She laughed and the next thing he knew she was slipping away, leaving him standing there hard and eager as she shimmied out of her undergarments.

This was a deliberate striptease, and he smiled as she kicked off her sandals and descended into the pool, a bold performance that had his blood pumping hard enough to make him overcome his every hesitation about the merits of a mud bath.

He followed, slogging into the cool mess until he was neck deep. Miranda piled her hair high on her head and sat on a built-in seat. She closed her eyes with a sigh, and he took advantage of the moment to find her leg and slide his foot behind her knee.

"You know, Troy, something occurred to me last night while I was talking with my grandfather."

"What's that?"

"He told me that my grandmother had tried to convince him to get help dealing with the aftereffects of his imprisonment. But he was so focused on his family's expectations of him, and his own, too, I think, that he tried to block out any reminders of the war instead."

"Not uncommon, especially after the conditions he endured in a concentration camp." Troy not only knew history, but was intimately acquainted with the risks servicemen and -women took on as part of the job. "Coping isn't easy, Miranda. The government provides assistance to rehabilitate servicemen physically and emotionally, but I don't know what was available in your grandfather's time."

"It wouldn't have mattered. My grandfather didn't want help. He told me it took him years to understand what happened, and by then he'd already sacrificed everything by pretending everything was fine."

She was in a reflective mood, reminding him again of how long it had been since she'd been this at ease and casual about how she felt. He stretched back against the wall, surprised how the velvety cool mud penetrated his muscles.

"What's bugging you about that?" he asked.

"Grandfather pushed everyone away. He felt like he'd failed because he wasn't perfect, and he blamed himself for everything that happened. By assuming all that responsibility, he never gave anyone a chance to be there to support him." She didn't open her eyes, just inhaled a sound like a sigh. "But he had a whole family that loved him. To this day, my mother sticks by him, but it doesn't matter how much she tries to love him if he doesn't let himself be loved."

"I hear another epiphany in there."

She laughed softly. "As a matter of fact, I think I've been doing the very same thing. Pushing the people who love me away because I'm so worried about being perfect."

"But you are perfect, Miranda."

She opened her eyes and looked at him, her expression melting. "I know you believe that, Troy, but it doesn't matter how perfect you think I am if I don't let myself believe it, too."

"And you haven't been." Not a question.

"No."

"Why?"

"I've been asking myself the same thing, and I think I've been living a self-fulfilling prophecy—expecting myself to be perfect and then feeling bad when I'm not. It's so stupid—"

"How can you say it's stupid?" Troy propelled himself away from the pool's edge and slogged through the mud to sit beside her. "You belong to a founding family in this town. You've got a legacy to live up to, and even the senator admitted that his family's expectations have always been high. Add that to the political involvement…" He exhaled heavily. "My point is your family situation has to be dealt with. Your aunt washed her hands of the whole thing. Victoria was on her way down that road, too. You and your mother have been toeing the line. That's a lot of pressure."

He slipped his arm around her, and she leaned her head against his shoulder, the only part of him not submerged in mud.

Burying his face in her hair, Troy savored the feel of her pressed against him. "We'll figure this out, Miranda. There are things I can do to remind you how perfect you are for me, just like there are things you can do to accept the reminders. It takes two of us. That's what marriage is all about."

"You're right." She nestled closer and pressed a kiss to his throat. "I need to tell you something."

And he knew they'd taken another important step when she shared everything that had been happening with his teammates' wives back home and her retreat from the problem.

Leaning back against the pool edge with her against him, he ran his hands down her arms and enjoyed the unfamiliar friction of the velvety mud against her skin.

"I want you to know that I understand why you didn't say anything about all this." He needed her to accept that she wasn't solely responsible, to know she wouldn't be alone again. "I've been having a few epiphanies myself lately, and I realized how I totally ignore what goes on while I'm away. I read what you post on the Web site and hear what you tell me on the phone, but it's not as if I've been participating. I leave you to handle everything and then bring me up to speed."

Tipping her face back, she stared up at him, frowning as though trying to comprehend what he'd said. "Troy, this isn't about anything you did. This is about *me* and the way I've chosen to handle things."

"If I was more involved, you might have felt more inclined to share."

"But you shouldn't have to worry about this trivial stuff while you're away. You've got a lot more important things to deal with while you're working."

"Our life together isn't trivial, Miranda." And he was appalled that she'd interpreted his lack of participation that way. "It's important to me."

She reached up to touch him, frowned at her mud-covered hand then pressed a kiss to his lips instead. "Shh. I know it is. That's not what I meant. I'm talking about the day-to-day things that come up. Remember my car and the telegram? You got dragged in from the desert for a decision I could have easily made myself. Once I understood that, I stopped bothering you—"

"Whoa, whoa, wait a second." He reached for her, slipping his muddy hands over her shoulders and forcing her to sit up and face him. He was missing something here, and he instinctively knew it was important.

"What are you talking about? What about your car and the telegram?"

She exhaled a sigh of exasperation. "Remember when I sent you that telegram because I needed to trade in my car?"

He nodded.

"You told me to deal with the situation. You said that you trusted me to make those kinds of decisions, and I didn't need to bother you with them."

Bother him? Her tone implied that he'd been pretty definite on the matter, and he dragged his memory for some recollection of what he'd said and how he might have said it.

Then he remembered the conga line of people who'd handled her telegram before it had finally reached him. Even the chaplain had read it to decide whether it qualified as an emergency. By the time he'd gotten Miranda on the phone, he hadn't been thrilled at being dragged out of a cave where he'd been on a recon mission to have her telegram delivered.

"Miranda, sending the telegram was never a problem. If I sounded annoyed, it wasn't because I was annoyed with you. The guys had to track me down in the desert. They'd all read it and were ragging on me. They didn't stop for weeks."

"I never meant to embarrass you," she said softly.

He gave an exasperated laugh. "You didn't. Suffice to say we get bored. Asking me if I'd called home to check on my wife a million times a day seemed funnier than it would have been otherwise."

He reached for her hands, slipped his fingers through hers and gave a squeeze. "Half of them were jealous because I have a gorgeous wife who sends me telegrams. I had no idea you'd take my reaction to heart, and I'm sorry. There's nothing about our life that I find trivial so I'm going to repeat what I said the other day and you have to believe it. I can't stop living when I'm away. I don't want to."

"Oh, so that's what that was all about?"

He nodded and pulled her close, their muddy bodies fitting together in a surprisingly sexy, gooey sort of way. "Let's agree that we'll both put forth some effort to communicate better while I'm away, Mrs. Knight."

"Agreed, Lieutenant Commander."

Then he held her, enjoying the companionable silence, the sluggish bubbling of the mud bath, the whisper of her breathing close to his ear.

He'd had no idea Miranda would take his reaction to her telegram so seriously, which warned him about reacting carelessly. Had he been thinking about his wife and not himself, he could have guessed that she would have responded by assuming more responsibility. But he hadn't been. He'd been letting her assume so much of the responsibility she'd been drowning in it.

There was a lesson here. He was half of a couple and he needed to start thinking like he was. It wouldn't be the easiest thing to do since he and Miranda spent so much time apart. Getting Miranda to not overload her plate wouldn't be easy, either, but if they were aware of the pitfalls, they could stay on top of them.

And that was when Troy realized he had a few things to fess up about, too.

"By the way, my mom thinks you're facing some

jealousy with those women back home," he said in an offhand tone, then held his breath and waited for the fallout.

Sure enough, Miranda pulled out of his arms and frowned so hard he hoped he had enough leverage to work his way out of this one. "Your *mom?* How would she know about any of this?"

"I called her. Since my wife hadn't filled me in on what was going on in her life, I was trying to figure it out for myself. I needed some help."

Now she was scowling. "Your *mom,* Troy? Why your *mom?*"

"I pieced together enough to get an idea of where I should start looking, but I needed someone to do a little nosing around. She's lived on more bases than I can count since she and Dad got married. She has connections all over the place."

"You asked your mother to use her connections to *nose around?*"

Troy was glad he'd decided to keep his revelations about colluding with Laura to himself for the time being. "I got the idea from your sister and Laura. Seemed like the thing to do at the time, since I'd already spent two weeks in the most romantic getaway trying to seduce you into telling me what was wrong."

He paused, pulling her back against him forcibly and hung on when she tried to get away.

"After you sprang Tease and Torture on me, I decided I'd better take action." Capturing her gaze, he willed her to see how much he meant what he said. "I won't take chances with you, Miranda. I love you too much."

Troy knew he'd played his card at exactly the right

time, because her eyes grew misty and her expression softened. She stopped resisting.

"Oh, Troy." With a laugh, she rested her head on his shoulder. "What makes your mother think the witchy wives are jealous?"

"The witchy wives?" He chuckled. "My mother knows you, and she says you wow people. Some women might feel threatened by that. Now, don't get me wrong, I happen to love this about you. In fact, it challenged me when we first met. I wanted to make you react."

She gave him a smile that told him she knew he was fast-talking to take the edge from his words. "Victoria said basically the same thing. She said it's been a nightmare trying to keep up with Mother and me, and I never had the slightest idea she felt that way."

"Did that prompt an epiphany?"

She nodded.

"I can see it." And he could. She was a tough act for anyone to follow, or compete with, as he suspected was the case with the *witchy wives*.

"You know, one thing I have figured out after talking to my grandfather is that I don't want to find myself in another situation where I'm on the outside looking in. I've never done this before and I haven't been very successful dealing with it. I have to learn how to let myself be included. If I don't share how I feel, there's no way anyone can know. It's my responsibility."

"You can start practicing on me. You can let your hair down and share whatever's on your mind and trust that I'll always be crazy in love with you and still think you're perfect."

"I'm *not* perfect."

"Oh, but you are, Mrs. Knight." He dragged his lips down the smooth curve of her cheek, worked his way toward her mouth. "You're perfect, *for me*. I need to convince you and you need to believe it."

"That sounds like an order, Lieutenant Commander." And when she tipped her mouth to his for a kiss, he knew everything would be okay.

"I won the bet, remember?" he whispered against her lips. "I want you to talk with my mother. She had some really solid suggestions for getting involved on base. If it helps any, she did say that wasn't easy."

"What kind of suggestions?"

"She mentioned a woman she knows who's been around a long time and can hook you up with some volunteer work. She's thinks it'll be a great way for you to get out and get to know people."

Sliding his hands around her hips, he dragged her onto his lap. "Mom gave her a call, and they both jumped on using your Web design skills to help out the youth club. I told her how great you are with kids. Or," he continued, "maybe now would be a good time to start law school. We're settled for a while. It's a thought."

"It is indeed." Snaking her arms around his neck, she squirmed around on his lap, a very deliberate attempt to make certain body parts rise to the occasion.

"I'll take that to mean you like my ideas."

"Mmm-hmm. They're good ideas."

"Glad you think so because we're done mud bathing. Let's go. I've got a prize with my name all over it."

"Is that another order?"

"It is. I'm done waiting. It's been torture."

Miranda bit his lower lip playfully. "You're the one who insisted on waiting."

"Only because you're worth the wait."

"Good to know. Now follow me." Suddenly, she slid off his lap, and Troy's pulse raced when she headed for the stairs.

"Did you forget that I'm the one in charge?" he asked.

"No, but I'm not done teasing you yet. You can have me if you can catch me." She shot him a smile that singed his brain cells. "But we'll have to rinse off the mud first."

Troy gave a laugh that echoed off the tile walls. "Your wish is my command, Mrs. Knight."

Chasing Miranda through the thick mud resembled more of a training maneuver than a mad dash to claim his prize, and she had the showerheads running full blast by the time he managed the top step.

Troy wasn't sure what happened next, but somehow they wound up rolling around on that slick tile floor, using the pulsing showerheads to wash away stubborn mud in some very private places. Next came a sexy water war, and from there, one thing led to another…

When he finally wrestled the sprayer from Miranda and trapped her in his arms, Troy knew he was going to score big claiming his reward, and he'd gotten his wish, too—Falling Inn Bed had worked its magic on them.

Epilogue

TAKING A DEEP BREATH, Miranda eased open the dressing room door only minutes before the Naughty Nuptials denouement was scheduled to begin. The guests were already being seated in the atrium, which had been decorated more lavishly than she'd ever seen it with lush blooms imported from South American hothouses and white doves flying through the trees up to the skylights overhead.

The day had dawned sunny and clear, the perfect day for a wedding, or two, and when she peeked inside the dressing room, she couldn't help but smile at the sight inside.

Victoria and Laura stood in front of the mirrors, outfitted to the nines in their finery, primping with makeup and hair.

"Now how do you make your hair stay shiny like that?" Victoria was asking. "Mine's gone nuts with all this humidity."

"Good genes," Laura replied dryly, and Victoria burst into laughter.

Miranda watched the exchange, surprised by the easiness between cousins who'd only known each other for a matter of weeks, and surprised by the emotion suddenly riding high in her throat at the sight of her sister's excitement.

Victoria had done exactly what she'd said she would do—she hadn't let anyone ruin her special day.

And Miranda was proud of her for that.

She wasn't so proud when Victoria caught sight of her in the mirror and her smile faded. "Miranda, you're here."

That question in her voice solidified Miranda's decision to make the effort to get closer to her sister. Las Vegas wasn't that far from San Diego, and with one generation of sisters making amends, she couldn't think of a more perfect time.

"Of course I'm here. You asked me to be your matron of honor, remember?"

She didn't get a chance to dwell on Victoria's surprise because Laura retreated from the mirror toward a side door.

"Don't go, Laura." A lifetime of history melted away on a newfound sense of purpose. "I need you both to come with me for a second."

Victoria frowned. "Where?"

"Our grooms can't see us, or it'll be bad luck," Laura said.

"Troy has your grooms locked up in the waiting area. They'll have to get past him to get to you, and I promise you my husband's well trained in armed combat. So don't worry."

She motioned them through the door. Both her brides looked puzzled, but the instant Laura saw her coworkers lined up like an honor guard blocking the doorways along the hallway, she said, "Uh-oh."

"Come on." The general manager flagged them to get moving. "Hurry or you'll miss it."

Miranda nodded, then looped her arms through each of the brides' and led them down the hallway. The maintenance supervisor brought a finger to his lips as they approached the entrance to the Wedding Wing, and Miranda forgot to breathe when they all peeked inside the lobby to watch some very special guests arrive.

Aunt Suzanne already stood inside, dressed in a lovely blue gown that complemented her creamy skin and shiny dark hair. She looked as breathless and nervous as Miranda felt.

The moment seemed to slow to a crawl when her mother and grandfather appeared, arms linked as they walked down the hallway from the main hotel. The sales director was with them, but she led them into the lobby, then retreated discreetly, slipping into the service corridor.

They stood there watching unobserved as her mother escorted her grandfather across the lobby to where Aunt Suzanne waited, and when they passed *The Falling Woman*, her grandfather stopped and looked up at it. Miranda's throat burned as she watched him lean heavily on his cane. The weight of so many lonely years and such hard truths were a visible burden, but she believed that with his daughters in his life again and the truth on the table, that they'd all start to heal.

Aunt Suzanne went to join them, and Miranda could see the glint of tears in her eyes as she rose on tiptoes to kiss her father's cheek. Then he took her hand, and together they proceeded toward the atrium. A family again.

Miranda didn't have the chance to urge her brides

back down the hall so they wouldn't be late for their own weddings. No sooner had their mothers disappeared inside the atrium then Victoria flung her arms around Miranda's neck. "You did it!"

"*We* did it." She hugged her sister back.

It was a good start.

And when Victoria finally let her go, Miranda extended her hand to Laura. "We'll let the past stay in the past?"

Laura took her hand. "Where it belongs. Thanks for all your help."

And that was it. The past was over, leaving the way cleared to the future.

Then she led them back down the hallway in time to take her place in the foyer for the walk down the aisle. The general manager cued her to wait as Laura's maid of honor made her entrance before Laura and her father. Then Miranda began her walk, leading the way for her teary-eyed sister.

Her sister wasn't the only one with teary eyes today, either. Miranda noticed her mother's moist gaze as she stood beside her father and sister.

Of course, Tyler's cameras were catching everything on tape, along with those from a local network. Victoria's photographer was snapping shots that she had no doubt would be plastered all over the paper tomorrow to show the town that the past had been put to bed today.

Who'd have guessed that the Naughty Nuptials would turn into such a family event? Not Miranda for sure, but she was very pleased with the turn of events as she stood beneath the lushly decorated archway, opposite Laura and Dale, and watched her sister walk down the aisle on her father's arm.

Adam stood nearby, and one glimpse at the look on his face—a look she'd seen often enough on Troy's face to recognize—and she knew that all she had to do was let herself believe Victoria would be happy. She might not understand instant engagements, but she did understand love. And there was no doubt that her sister and her almost brother-in-law were head over heels.

And they weren't the only ones. Miranda gazed into the sea of guests to find her own husband, who looked so impossibly handsome dressed as a civilian in a custom suit that hugged the lines of his impressive body that still had the power to make her tingle with just a glance. She saw everything she felt for him mirrored in his clear green eyes and knew without any doubt that he loved her more than anything.

Because they were perfect for each other.

And Miranda smiled, a smile to assure him that she'd let herself believe it. No matter what happened in the future, no matter what life dealt them, she was committed to dealing with it *together.*

She was done keeping secrets, except perhaps for some sexy secrets. If he could surprise her with a dual-temperature vibrator and a mobile sexy sheet party, she'd do her part to keep the celebration going. She'd already given him a sneak preview by proving just how pleasurable mud baths could be.

And Miranda had found sharing her secrets…*liberating.* When one got caught up in the moment, one's orgasms stayed right where they belonged.

So she decided then and there that she'd always be

ready for a sexy adventure with the man she loved with all her heart. And to prove it, she mouthed the vows to him as the brides and grooms spoke theirs.

This vacation hadn't been anything like she'd expected. But, then, things didn't always turn out as planned. Life could be like that. Sometimes miracles happened, and things turned out even better.

HARLEQUIN® *Blaze*™

When three women go to a lock-and-key
party to meet sexy singles, they never
expect to find their perfect matches....

#166 HARD TO HANDLE
by Jamie Denton
January 2005

#170 ON THE LOOSE
by Shannon Hollis
February 2005

#174 SLOW RIDE
by Carrie Alexander
March 2005

Indulge in these three blazing hot stories today!

Lock & Key
Unlock the possibilities...

On sale at your favorite retail outlet.

HBLK04

If you enjoyed what you just read,
then we've got an offer you can't resist!

Take 2 bestselling love stories FREE!

Plus get a FREE surprise gift!

Clip this page and mail it to Harlequin Reader Service®

IN U.S.A.	IN CANADA
3010 Walden Ave.	P.O. Box 609
P.O. Box 1867	Fort Erie, Ontario
Buffalo, N.Y. 14240-1867	L2A 5X3

YES! Please send me 2 free Blaze™ novels and my free surprise gift. After receiving them, if I don't wish to receive anymore, I can return the shipping statement marked cancel. If I don't cancel, I will receive 4 brand-new novels each month, before they're available in stores! In the U.S.A., bill me at the bargain price of $3.99 plus 25¢ shipping and handling per book and applicable sales tax, if any*. In Canada, bill me at the bargain price of $4.47 plus 25¢ shipping and handling per book and applicable taxes**. That's the complete price and a savings of at least 10% off the cover prices—what a great deal! I understand that accepting the 2 free books and gift places me under no obligation ever to buy any books. I can always return a shipment and cancel at any time. Even if I never buy another book from Harlequin, the 2 free books and gift are mine to keep forever.

150 HDN DZ9K
350 HDN DZ9L

Name	(PLEASE PRINT)	
Address	Apt.#	
City	State/Prov.	Zip/Postal Code

Not valid to current Harlequin Blaze™ subscribers.

Want to try two free books from another series?
Call 1-800-873-8635 or visit www.morefreebooks.com.

* Terms and prices subject to change without notice. Sales tax applicable in N.Y.
** Canadian residents will be charged applicable provincial taxes and GST.
  All orders subject to approval. Offer limited to one per household.
® and ™ are registered trademarks owned and used by the trademark owner and or its licensee.

BLZ04R   ©2004 Harlequin Enterprises Limited.

e**HARLEQUIN**.com

The Ultimate Destination for Women's Fiction

Becoming an eHarlequin.com member is easy,
fun and **FREE!** Join today to enjoy great benefits:

- **Super savings** on all our books, including
  members-only discounts and offers!

- Enjoy **exclusive online reads**—FREE!

- Info, tips and **expert advice** on writing
  your own romance novel.

- FREE romance **newsletters,**
  customized by you!

- Find out the latest on your
  favorite authors.

- Enter to win exciting **contests
  and promotions!**

- Chat with other members in our
  community message boards!

To become a member,
visit www.eHarlequin.com today!

INTMEMB04R

The world's bestselling romance series.

HARLEQUIN®
Presents
Seduction and Passion Guaranteed!

Mamma Mia!

They're tall, dark...and ready to marry!

Don't delay. Order the next story in
this great new miniseries...pronto!

On sale in January
THE ITALIAN'S
TOKEN WIFE
by *Julia James* #2440

Furious at his father's ultimatum, Italian millionaire
Rafaello di Viscenti vows to marry the first woman he sees—
Magda, a single mother desperately trying to make ends meet
by doing his cleaning! Rafaello's proposal comes with a
financial reward, so Magda has no choice but to accept....

**Pick up a Harlequin Presents® novel and you will enter a world
of spine-tingling passion and provocative, tantalizing romance!**

Available wherever Harlequin Books are sold.

www.eHarlequin.com

HPTITW0105

Look for more

...before you say "I do."

In January 2005 have a taste of

#165 A LICK AND A PROMISE

by **Jo Leigh**

Enjoy the latest sexual escapades
in the hottest miniseries

Only from Blaze

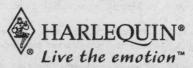

www.eHarlequin.com   HBMTD0105